FALLING INTO A SECOND CHANCE

ALIE GARNETT

For those who love this series as much as I do.

<h1 style="text-align:center">CHAPTER ONE</h1>

THE MORNING BELL had not yet rung, and the hallway at Harry Truman High School was still full of kids passing time. Agatha Christie Lovely looked over her domain; she was a senior, so therefore, she ruled the school. Yes, she had been named after the famed mystery author. No, she did not actually rule the school, but she finally had a place in it. After spending every day of her high school career at HTHS, on the last week of the last year, she had a place. Because she had a boyfriend. Finally!

Not just any boy either, Christopher Lowell. He'd been her crush for years at Harry Truman High School, and during her time at Ben Franklin Middle School, and even before that at PS12 Elementary School. Agatha had fallen in love with Christopher in third grade when he had sat at the table right next to her with his blond curls and told her he liked her drawing. Even then, he knew the way to a woman's heart.

Just because she had fallen in love with him in the third grade didn't mean he fell for her or even noticed her. In the fourth grade, he had accidentally slammed his locker into her face, which got her three stitches in the forehead. Christopher had given her a get-well card but had spelled her name wrong, which had made her mad. But he personally handed her the card, so she forgave him quickly. Sure, "Christie" and "Chrissy" were close, but not really. Both were very different from Agatha, a name she refused to use in school.

By fifth grade, he had remembered her again. Due to their last names, Lovely and Lowell, their lockers were always side by side, and he would say hi to her. He would look right into her eyes, because they were the same height, and say, "Hey Chrissy." So maybe he remembered her name wrong even though it was written on her locker, but he remembered her. It was enough to make her stomach queasy, in a good way.

In sixth grade, they moved to middle school, and Christopher started to call her Christie every day. He had also grown when she had not. She was short, and he had to look down at her. That was the year he had gotten really good at football while she quit sports altogether. It was also the year her dad married a new wife and then took off, leaving her stepmom in charge. Seeing Chris at their lockers every day was the only thing that stayed constant for her that year—a constant she desperately needed.

Sixth grade was also the first year that kids were not required to give Valentine's cards to everyone in their class. Christie still did because her stepmom bought them and forced her to fill them out. To her delight, she had gotten one from Christopher, football star Christopher.

When seventh grade rolled around, having her locker next to Chris had gotten to be old hat. He only accidentally slammed her head with his locker four times that year, but no stitches. And each time he apologized profusely. He told her he didn't always see her since he was still getting taller and she stayed short, something she didn't need to be reminded of. There were no valentines that year for either of them. It was also the first year she became serious about getting over her crush and moving on. After all, she was almost a teenager, and there was quite a few cute boys in school. But he still flashed her knee-weakening smiles every once in a while, and everyone else was instantly forgotten.

In eighth grade, a steady stream of girls loitered around his locker, making getting to hers almost impossible. Usually, she didn't take any of her books with her to class because she couldn't get to them. It was that year, on September 19th, that he told her she should let her hair grow out, that he thought she'd be cuter with long hair. One thing women don't tell you is that hair takes forever to grow, no matter what home remedies their sisters tried on them. In the end, she came to the conclusion that she had slow-growing hair and evil sisters. Once again, no valentine.

Finally, when she'd moved on to high school, she thought that her Chris days were finally behind her. But no, the entire year of ninth grade, they were again locker buddies. Every week his locker would be decorated by the cheerleaders. How it helped him play better, Christie never knew, but every week there were steamers and signs everywhere—except for the two times they decorated hers by mistake. A new school meant a new name: Chris. Sure, it was not the name her family called her, and it was the same as his, but Chris and Chris would be so cute on a Christmas card, and everyone would just call them the Chrises. Chris didn't notice her new, longer hair, but he did say "Hey Chris" all the time. He liked it. Since she was finally in high school, she was able to take an actual art class, and she found her place in a place she had never been comfortable before.

Tenth grade was a bust. Her older twin sisters, Lucy and Mabel, were seniors and involved in everything. They routinely forced Christie to go to football games with them, which wasn't actually forcing because Chris was playing. Christie thought he was so cute in the blue uniform. He would still say "Hey Chris" to her every day and would even do it when they weren't by their lockers, recognizing her in the wild! That was all he would say to her, but then again, she wasn't trying all that hard to start conversations with him. He had more than enough girls around who were trying to get his attention. Christie had started painting and drawing a lot more. It had always been her passion, but now suddenly she was getting direction, and people were noticing her works. So, she would stay up late and then wake up late the next day, leaving her no time to do a lot of girly stuff in the morning. He was still growing, and she had finally realized she would never grow again.

Eleventh grade was a big year for her because she took a few more art classes. Chris still said hello to her every day, but she had started to go by Christie again. She enjoyed that Chris was all muscly that year. For the first time, there was a new student whose name fell between theirs, separating their lockers for half the year before she left, which then meant they had an empty locker that they shared. Both knew the combination, and both stored their coats in it. Every day she got to smell him on her coat as she walked home from school. Most of her classmates thought she had gone goth that year, but really, Christie just liked to wear black and happened to have black hair. Never did she wear black makeup or much leather. She was just herself and accepted herself easily, which to others, looked gothic.

For their senior year, they were back to being locker neighbors, but with no extra locker for storage, and the cheerleaders never decorated the wrong locker again. Chris spent most of the year dating Savannah J, who he had taken to junior and senior prom. Christie spent the year watching Savannah J's hands slide all over Chris. He still said "Hey Chris" to her, and in science class, they ended up being lab partners all year. Tuesdays and Thursdays, they spent an hour together talking and laughing, not doing overly well in science. He was a jock, and she was an artist, and they were destined for the C plus grade they got. By the end of the year, she was considered them friends and knew she was just as much in love with him as she was in the third grade, but now they were more than strangers. Sure, he didn't love her, but he knew her.

In late March, a new girl showed up at the high school. Unlike Christie, she was absolutely a goth. Dayle Sullivan had taken Christie under her wing from the moment she sat down next to her in Math class. From then on, they went to every party they heard about. Dayle was completely different from any of her other friends and made Christie way more outgoing than she ever had been. She also encouraged Christie to apply to art school for the next year, the one she got into. It was a dream come true.

On May 1st, Savannah J broke up with Chris. He was devastated, but girls huddled at his locker en masse. In science lab, he told her that he was going to remain single and play the field for the rest of high school, the entire month left of it.

Christie began running into Chris at all the parties Dayle dragged her to. Not that she approached him since he had his friends and tons of girls surrounding him after the break-up. The last Friday before graduation, Christie was drinking one of the horrid mixed drinks at a party. Whoever was in charge should be fired because they were not even close to actual drinkable combinations.

She had quickly learned at these parties that her taste for alcohol was a bit more sophisticated than her peers. But then again, thanks to three older sisters and some very lax rules at home, she had been drinking for years already.

But thanks to a good buzz, she did what it had taken ten years to do: Christie asked Chris to dance. He had shrugged off his friends and had danced with her. Her, Agatha Christie Lovely, with long, black stick-straight hair and dressed from head to toe black. The song was "Hero" by Enrique Iglesias, and it was absolutely perfect. Her feelings had been summed up in one song. Maybe it was her buzz or finally being in his arms, but Christie knew that nobody else would ever be able to compete with him in her eyes.

It must have been the same for him because when the song ended, he kissed her on the lips. Right there in the middle of some house on Kendel Street, she got her kiss from Chris Lowell, captain of the football team, tall with curly blond hair and baby blue eyes. It was everything she had dreamed it would be, including a bit of tongue, which she was absolutely ready for.

As they kissed, his friends pulled him away, laughing. He laughed too as he went, leaving her heart broken in the middle of the dance floor alone, the butt of their joke.

Not wanting to spend another moment as the punchline of a joke, she went looking for Dayle. Without success on the main floor, she found her on the second floor, making out at the end a hallway with someone Christie didn't recognize, so she took her car keys and headed back to the main part of the house to get away from all these people. She hadn't liked most of them sober, so why would she want to be with them drunk?

As she neared the stairs, a bedroom door opened suddenly, and Chris Lowell was standing there looking at her in surprise. With a wave, she gave their usual greeting, this time half-heartedly, "Hey Chris."

With a cocky grin, he took one step out of the room, grabbed her arm, and pulled her back inside with him. The room was decorated in blues and browns and looked like it had been pulled from a magazine.

"Hey Chris," he whispered back as his arms went around her.

She had no time to answer before his lips were on hers again. There was no song playing; it was just them alone. Everything he asked for, she willingly gave him in that perfect bedroom. They messed up the bed, and Christie couldn't bring herself to regret it. It had been the magical first time she had dreamed of.

After it was done, he told her that they should date, that he really liked her and thought she was special. He'd said everything she had always dreamed of him saying to her. He had helped her dress and had walked her to her car. The party had broken up, and most people were gone by then.

They had kissed at the Jeep, and she had driven home as his girl-friend. Saturday and Sunday were spent hiding her excitement from her sisters and stepmom, not ready to share her fortune with them yet. She wanted to have one date under her belt before telling everyone. She walked into Harry Truman High School Monday morning as his girlfriend.

Chris was leaning against his locker with his back to her, talking to his two friends, like she had seen many times over the years. Putting her backpack in the locker, she listened to his deep baritone.

"Christie? What about her?" Her head snapped up at her name.

"I heard you were dating the weirdo," the blond friend said, shifting so she couldn't see anything but his back. He must have known she was there but didn't want Chris to know.

"No way, man. You aren't dating her, are you? She's weird." The other guy shook his head in disgust and looked right at her.

Christie bit her lip and continued to listen. What was Chris going to say? Would he tell them he thought that she was special, special enough to date? Would he tell them that they were dating? Would he say anything?

"Come on, guys, it was just sex," Chris's baritone rumbled, taking Christie's breath away.

"Did she paint you in the nude?" One of them chuckled.

"No, she didn't do any of her stupid painting, just sex. Hot sex." His words broke her heart.

"So you're not dating?" the blond asked again, his eyes looking right at her, causing her to look away to hide the pain his words caused.

"I would never date her; she's a stupid art geek. Fuck her, yes, but date her? Never." He laughed with his friends ... at her.

"You should tell her that, Lowell. There she is," the blond pointed out.

Christie suddenly grabbed her bag out of her locker and turned from them. Without looking behind her, she walked away from her locker and her locker mate since the third grade. Ten years she had wanted nothing but his attention, but not like this. She would never be the butt of his jokes again, never.

Walking out of Harry Truman High School the last time into the morning sun, she decided she was done with Chris, Christopher, and Christie. From now on, she was Agatha and would never be that naïve, trusting girl again. Agatha Lovely would never let someone that close to her heart again.

CHAPTER TWO

SEVEN YEARS later

THE REALIZATION that your sister hated you came slowly for some. Harper had always been one of Agatha's favorite sisters, at least until today. Today she was making her serve hors d'oeuvres during some kind of football thing, and her hors d'oeuvre was served in a cup. So now she would have to round up all the stupid cups afterwards.

"Smile, Ag," Harper said to her with a smile of her own. Which sister's smile was more fake, Agatha didn't know. Harper was her physical opposite: blonde hair and bubbly, outgoing, and ambitious. Hence owning her own catering company before thirty.

"I quit," Agatha said and looked at the platter again.

"No quitting; you're family," Lucy said from behind her. The two had started this business over two years before and were doing very well, which meant Agatha was forced to work these stupid events all the time.

"Today, a football player has been swapped by one NFL team for another," Harper stated in her speech, something she always started these events with.

"Traded, not swapped," Lucy corrected, causing Harper to glare at her.

"I *said* traded. Anyway, this is a press event to tell the city about their new player. Or something like that," Harper explained. "And they have chosen Lovely Catering to supply the food."

"Football?" Agatha groaned.

"This is big, Agatha, so big. Over a hundred people big, so many contacts and potential business. And TV stations will be here!" Lucy squealed, and Harper joined in. Maby and Agatha did not. Slave labor didn't get excited about working, no matter how high-profile the event.

"Can you even believe it? And Christopher Lowell is the player. *The* Christopher Lowell," Harper said, as if sports were something the sisters talked about, ever.

Agatha looked up from all the little cups on her tray at her sister. Could it be her Christopher Lowell? Big, tall, muscular, and mouth-wateringly handsome? She hadn't heard anything about Chris since she last saw him in the hallway by their lockers, not that she had spent any time looking. Ending her school career that day, she never went back. Her diploma arrived in the mail a month later. Now after seven years, she was completely over him. It had to be a different guy anyway.

"I remember him at Harry Truman. He was a starter before we even graduated," Lucy said. "Wasn't he your age, Ag?"

Looking up at her sister in fake confusion, she said, "I don't remember. My graduating class was big."

Suddenly, she was glad she had never told anyone about it. Not even about having a crush on him.

"Yeah, I only remember him because he had a sister my age. Cara, I think that was her name. Do you remember, Lucy?" Maby asked her twin, who just shook her head.

"You don't remember the sister, but the brother you can't forget?" Harper teased her.

"Hey, they were part of the rich group. I was not part of that group," Maby said.

"Probably why I don't remember him either," Agatha lied.

Lucy looked at her closely, too closely. What was she seeing? Lucy and Maby were only two years older than she was. Did Lucy remember the terrible crush she had had on Christopher?

"What?" Agatha demanded.

"You got your hair cut. Should that one part be standing up?" Lucy pointed to the side of her head.

"Yes, it's edgy." She tried not to touch her hair; she didn't want to wash her hands again. But she wondered if it still looked like it had hours before or if it was droopy now. Not that she could do anything about it now. And besides, if it looked too bad, Harper would never allow her to work that night.

"I know that, but you should maybe rethink it," Lucy said, reaching out to touch it.

"Hey, hands off, Luce." Agatha dodged away from her sister.

This morning when she had sat in the salon chair, she had wanted edgy and different, but by lunch, she was no longer happy with her hair. Now she had to live with it until it grew out. Tomorrow she wouldn't spike it, but since the stylist had that morning, she would leave it today. Agatha couldn't pull off edgy but consoled herself that not everyone could.

"Okay, are we ready?" Harper asked as they all picked up a tray. It sounded like people were there. And if there were people, they would want tiny bites of food delivered to them one piece at a time.

Harper started out, followed by the twins, with Agatha bringing up the rear. Glancing at the clock before she left, she saw it was 5 p.m. The event was scheduled to last until 10 p.m., and then at midnight, she was off to her real job, bartending at the Sunrise Tavern. It was a shitty job, but at least it paid, and there were tips.

Tomorrow was Monday morning, and at 10 a.m. she was going to meet with an actual book publisher, Abbot & Merchant. It had taken her weeks to get this meeting to show them the illustrations and mock-ups for a book she had been working on. It was a children's book she had originally drawn for Violet when she was a baby. But Agatha wanted more than her sister to see the books; she wanted to share them with the world. Tomorrow she would get her first chance to make that happen. Even right now, with hours before the meeting, she was nervous her work wouldn't be enough.

Out in the crowded room, she traced circular path, avoiding her sisters so that they were not at the same place. It took coordination and strategy to make the food distribution seem flawless.

It was on her first circle of the room that she saw Christopher Lowell. He had filled out even more over the past five years, and he looked more grown up. No longer was he the young boy she had stared at every day. Now he was all man and all muscle. The blond, wavy hair was just short stubble now. He was in jeans and a thin T-shirt, and she could see the muscles in his legs, arms, and on his chest.

Agatha couldn't take her eyes off him, at least until she ran into an old man and almost dropped her tray. She was so proud of herself for saving it. Agatha scored one in the "don't drop food on people" game, which was important—she didn't need to get in trouble with her sister today.

Christopher's brown eyes never left the TV screen that was showing clips of him playing for his previous team and some of the team he was going to play for. He didn't talk to anyone or eat anything. But he did drink, beer after beer all evening.

After only fifteen minutes, she had decided he was not going to recognize her, and she was able to relax. He didn't remember her or care about her if he did. But of course, he was the big football star now, and she was a waiter. Somehow it seemed their lives hadn't changed since high school; he was still the star, and she was still nothing. Seven years hadn't been long enough to change that.

From talk around the room, she had found out he had been traded against his will. He had been happy about it, but it seemed the team he was now on was not. So, when they had the chance, they traded him. He didn't seem afraid to show that he wasn't happy either.

As the night came to an end, Agatha went back to the kitchen to find Harper packing her supplies and dishes into big totes. With a sigh, she went to help her oldest sister. The job usually wasn't over until hours after the event due to the cleanup.

"You go, Ag. You have to work tonight." Harper waved her off.

"Thanks, Harps. See you tomorrow." She turned away from her sister. Though they lived in the same house, they would not see one another for the rest of the night. Harper and Lucy would stay and clean up until about the time Agatha needed to be at the bar.

Slipping through the event space, Agatha was excited to get an hour to herself before she had to be to work again. Maybe she would take a walk around the waterfront since she had already paid for parking.

She was out the door without anyone noticing, heading down the hallway toward the elevator. As she passed the restrooms, a very drunk Chris Lowell came out, slowly swaying.

His brown eyes looked at her and he grinned. "Hey, Chris."

With effort, she hid the smile his words of recognition caused her, but she responded one more time for old times' sake, "Hey, Chris," and walked away from him. Being a big football star and all, he probably wouldn't remember their meeting in the morning anyway. But now she would.

Pushing the down button at the elevator, she almost jumped out of her skin when he said from right behind her, "Nice hair."

Touching it now, she had forgotten about the new cut. "Thanks."

The doors swished open, and she walked into the elevator. He followed and said, "Fuck, you're hot."

"Thanks," she replied, not really knowing how to answer. She leaned into the wall of the elevator, realizing she kind of liked drunk Chris. One well-directed smile still made it easy for her to forgive him of anything.

"I want to fuck you," he whispered as he leaned into her, making her feel small and delicate.

"You don't even know my name." She let herself smell him again. He smelled the same as her jacket had all those years before.

Just being near him turned her mind to mush and smoothed the rough memories of the past. Knowing she should stop him and making it happen were two different things. She was with him right now, and he wanted to be with her again. What would be the harm in taking things further? After all, it was her choice. She knew better than to think it was more than right now. She wouldn't let her heart get involved.

"We're both Chrises." His tongue ran over her ear, sliding over earring after earring.

When the door opened, she tried to move, she really did. But his tongue had left her ear and was running over her neck. His hand reached over and pushed a button, and suddenly, her attention left the elevator door and focused on where his tongue would go next.

CHAPTER THREE

Fᴜᴄᴋ, he hated hangovers. Why did he have to drink so much that his head was throbbing? Rolling over, he wondered if he could even remember the press conference but realized he couldn't. With a groan, he opened his eyes to the bright room, then shut them again.

Christopher Lowell was twenty-five and should have easily known how to hold his liquor, but smiling and trying to act happy about ending up with the wrong team had made him reach for drink after drink. Yes, he should be happy just to be on a team still, but it wasn't the team he had loved playing for. They had decided they didn't love him.

Opening his eyes again, he saw the back of her head. Short black hair standing on end, the strands all pointing in different directions. But the sides were very short. He couldn't remember a thing about her. That should make him ashamed of what happened, but it wasn't the first time, and it wouldn't be the last. Women were easy when you played a sport like football at the level he did.

She was probably naked based on the creamy white shoulder that was peeking out from under the covers. He had a type, and short, black-haired chicks were not it. Weird hair usually did nothing for him either.

Chris had been dating tall blonds as long as he could remember. Never once had he strayed away from that mold, and he didn't see himself starting now. But it seemed that while drunk, he had wanted a taste of something else. Something completely different.

Leaning up on an elbow, Chris leaned over, realizing he wanted to see what that something else looked like. Now he could see that she had a mohawk and more metal in her ears than he thought possible. Her nose oddly didn't have anything pierced, but it was cute and buttony. Her pink lips were curved up in a light smile as she slept.

She stretched, and the cover slid down. Her breast came into view, nice sized with dark nipples that begged to be touched. So, he did, with a light caress.

The woman bolted upright and looked around the room. What she saw was enough to send her out from under the covers and running around the room naked, looking for her clothes. For such a little package, she was glorious to look at in the nude. Even though she was skin and bones, he enjoyed watching her search the room for whatever she had worn yesterday. He would be no help because he couldn't remember how they got to the room, much less where she had lost her clothes. Or his, for that matter.

After two circles around the room, her brown eyes glared at him as she demanded, "Where the fuck are my clothes?"

"I don't know. Bathroom?" He pointed to it, as if she hadn't actually already looked there, but he was rewarded by another view of her bare ass. It was a very nice ass.

She stomped into the room and came out again, empty-handed and still naked. "Oh, fuck. Is it 9:45?"

Not looking away from her breasts, Chris said, "Yup."

She rubbed her face with her hands and then over her pointy hair, swearing a lot. She stomped out of the bedroom of the suite and into the living room. She didn't come back, and he missed her nakedness in his life.

After a few minutes, he heard the door open and close. Was she gone? Not that he cared; she was just a drunk fuck. She was nobody that meant anything to him … they never were.

Getting up, he walked into the living room of the suite in case she hadn't left. He could use a hangover fuck if she was still around, but the room was empty. Walking back into the bedroom, he saw a piece of paper on the dresser and picked it up. All it said was his name on it: Chris. But it wasn't his writing, it was fancy, girly writing. The dark-haired chick must have written it, though he couldn't remember her doing it or even why she would have.

Sitting on the bed, he looked at the paper. Chris. Short, black-haired Chris. Flopping onto his back, he suddenly remembered her from the party. Chris Lovely, artsy Chris who he couldn't ever remember not knowing.

Every day he was at school, she was there. In class, by their lockers, or even hanging out with her friends across the schoolyard. Then senior year and everything that happened, from getting to know her to letting her go. She had been there, a constant he had relied on until she was gone.

Yelling curse words to the ceiling in anger, he had just fucked up with Chris Lovely again. Drunk Chris had known it was her, but sober Chris had just let her walk away. Again. This time he hadn't even been trying to impress his friends that led her to leaving; it had been his own stupidity.

And now, just like back then, he had no way to find her. He didn't know where she lived then or now. He had fucked up again. Should he have his agent find her? He could, easily. So much easier than what a high school kid could do. Except he was leaving town and wouldn't be back much anyway.

Closing his eyes, he wondered if he had been smart enough to have at least apologized to her for being a dick in high school. He hoped so.

It was better to just leave it as it was. A drunk fuck, because he was doing exactly what he had always dreamed: be a football star. She was nothing to him anyway, just some chick from his past.

CHAPTER FOUR

Eighteen months later

"So, your retirement plan is to flip houses?" Carter Lowell sat behind the desk their father had always sat at. At twenty-three, he shouldn't look as comfortable behind the desk as he did. But then again, he had been there for a few years now. Chris's brother had grown up while he had been away, and he was now more of an adult than Chris himself was.

"Yes, I just want to do something with my hands," Chris tried to explain his plans for the future, plans he hadn't thought he would have to worry about for decades. But a knee injury had changed that in an instant.

"Writing up insurance policies is using your hands." Carter shot him a grin and lifted his hands from his desk. His younger brother was close to fifty pounds lighter and half a foot shorter than himself. Carter had never been athletic like Chris. What they did share was blond hair and a last name.

"Not what I was thinking. You're doing great here; I would just mess it up." His brother had taken over the insurance firm after their father's sudden death three years before. Chris knew he should help his brother, but he had never wanted an office job. He never wanted to do what his father had done.

"I could always use help," Carter admitted, though Chris couldn't see himself trapped behind a desk.

"Maybe after I do this house. It's amazing. Just wait until you see how great it will look once it is done." Chris couldn't hide his excitement. Though he had never actually done any construction, he knew it was going to be easy and fun. That and hopefully it would take his mind off the fact that he was done with the sport he loved.

"Are you sure you're not getting in over year head?" Carter asked in concern.

Chris ran his hands through his blond, wavy hair, trying to sound more confident than he felt. "No, I can handle it." No way was he going to admit he didn't know what he was doing to his younger brother.

"Can your body?" Carter asked the question Chris wasn't sure of himself.

"The new knee shouldn't be an issue." Chris tapped the thing that had caused him so much pain over the last year. During the first game after being traded, he had torn his knee so bad he would never play again. It was supposed to be the season he proved himself, and one game in it was over. So much hard work for so little reward. Without football, he had no idea who he was.

Carter leaned back in his chair. "I don't think that is how it works, but I won't stop you, not that I could." It was the truth.

"Thanks. I never wanted to be what Dad was," Chris admitted. But to be honest, it wasn't selling insurance that he didn't want to do; it was the fear of turning into the same all-around dick that his father had been. They stopped getting along years before the man died. In fact, they never spoke after his parent's divorce when he was eighteen. Not that his dad hadn't reveled in Chris's football career, taking credit for his son's ability whenever possible.

"When do you start?" Carter wanted to know.

"I'm heading over there right now to take another look and figure out what I need."

"Well, have fun, and come help me if you get bored." Carter chuckled. They had never been the same type of person. Despite that, they always got along.

Walking out of his father's insurance firm, Chris headed toward the pickup he had bought just so that he could work on the house. And every other house after it, because this was going to be his future. He wasn't concerned that the house was old and would need a lot of work because he had time and money to spare. Between his one year in the NFL and everything his father had left him, he was doing okay.

The house renovation was mostly to take his mind off how his life was not going how he had ever wanted it to go. It was a five-bedroom, three-bathroom distraction.

It was only a short drive to the Allering neighborhood where the old, big houses were. Since he was young, he wanted to be a part of something that would last for centuries. Now he was going to live that dream, for a month or so at least. Then he would move on to another.

After a slow walk-through with his pen and paper in hand, he left his beautiful old house and walked right into an old lady standing on his porch. She was nothing less than eighty years old in her jogging suit and was happy to see him. Her gray hair was curly, and he wondered if she had cookies somewhere.

"Hello, I'm Nelly, and I live next door," she said and pointed to the white house next to him.

"I'm Chris, and I just brought this old lady." He pointed behind him and winced since the lady on his porch was old.

She either didn't notice the slip-up or was letting him slide because her smile didn't falter as she went on. "I know. We're all excited to see Hilda's house go to a young person. We're getting more and more young people lately."

"Do you know all the neighbors?" He, too, looked up and down the street and saw nobody outside.

"Of course." She turned around. "Patty and Mike live there, Russ and Sonia live there, then it's the Cramer's—they're odd—then it's just Agatha in the next house—all the others are gone now. Last is the Mortin's."

"Well, it sounds like a fun neighborhood," he said with a grin.

"It is. When do you move in?"

"I don't know. I have some things I have to get fixed first."

"Okay, I'll keep my eye out for you moving in then." She turned and walked away.

Chris looked at the house across the street and tried to remember if it belonged to the odd Cramers or Agatha. Either way, he didn't care. If he met people, he met people. He had friends and didn't need a neighborhood full of them.

With as friendly as Nelly was, he was excited to be in the neighborhood. This was his first step in his new life.

CHAPTER FIVE

"MANIC MONDAY" by The Bangles suddenly started to play throughout the house. Though Agatha couldn't hear the speakers on the main floor, she knew it was ringing throughout that floor also. She sang along as the words began, though she had never had the panic of being late for a job on Monday morning—or any morning for that matter. Her entire work career had been focused on nights. Waitressing, bartending…. At one time, she'd even been a night manager at a hotel. She was a night person.

There was nothing better than to crawl into bed as the sun came up, pull the covers over her head, and sleep until noon, or well past noon if there was enough silence. She would do it every day if given the opportunity, but she no longer worked odd hours for little pay and hope that there would be tips. Her only job now was as a waiter for her sisters' catering business. It sucked, but neither of her sisters would fire her, and she couldn't walk away from them. Some weeks it was the only time she saw them anymore.

Just one year ago, they had all been living here in the big boxy house they had been raised in. Sure, the oldest sister, Harper, was thirty, and the youngest, Buzz, was twenty-five at the time, but they all had bounced back to living together with Mom. Mom had been a bubbly thirty-five at the time and loved her stepkids as much as she loved the two she had borne herself.

Last year her stepmom had finally landed the love of her life. After years of pining for Harrison and oddly already having two children together, he finally noticed the perky blonde who worked in his office. They had dated for a short time and had married within a few months. Sera Lovely had started the great Lovely Fall, which had led to all four of her sisters finding a man in quick succession. Agatha was the last man standing, in the house and in the game of love.

Laying the hunter green pencil down, she looked over her drawing of a rabbit and a donkey talking. She knew what they were saying but hadn't added the words yet. The illustration looked like she had imagined it, which wasn't always the case. Sometimes her pictures came out wonky, and she had to redraw them.

Pushing away from her desk, she surveyed her domain. She'd had this bedroom since she was ten when sleeping in the same room with her sister Buzz became too much. One afternoon after school, she had dragged her mattress and all her worldly possessions up to the attic, and nobody had said a word. Of course, her real mom had been gone for years by then, and her dad didn't care much about any of his kids, so he didn't say anything.

Her bed was covered with stark white sheets and bedding. It was a dim room and needed the white linen to bring in the light. For years she had slept on black sheets, but as she grew up, she'd changed them to white. But she no longer slept in that bed unless she couldn't make it down the stairs to the master bedroom. Since her sisters had slowly moved out of the house and in with boyfriends, fiancé's, or husbands, Agatha had claimed the largest room as her own.

Still singing along with the song, Agatha headed down the flight of stairs to the second floor into the room she slept in now and grabbed the brightly colored box from the dresser. The box had been there in the closet for three weeks, until today waiting for today. In this room, her bedding was walnut brown and mint green, and she had loved it when she had seen it online a few months before.

Box in hand, she headed down the next flight of stairs to the main floor as another song about Monday came on. With a loud voice, she requested the little computer assistant to turn it off. She loved technology that kept her on time, because clocks had never been her thing. Many jobs had she lost because she forgot to go into work, too busy drawing or sleeping. More than once, a sister had yelled at her that she was missing a family function because she was drawing or sleeping. Now that they had all moved out, she spent all her time drawing or sleeping, except from 3 to 5 p.m. on weekdays.

Leaving the package on the kitchen counter, she grabbed a pop from the fridge and went through the big house again to the front door. Across the large wraparound porch, she skittered down the steps and grabbed the mail, sitting on the top step to wait.

At 3:10 p.m., Violet and Emmaline would get off the bus four blocks down and walk to her, passing their parents' new house as they went. Sera and Harrison worked until after 5 p.m., sometimes later. Most days, Emma would just go home, and Violet would walk alone, but some days, Emma wanted something to eat, and Agatha would feed them.

Flipping through the letters that had come that day, she saw bill, bill, paycheck. She still couldn't believe that she got paid to draw. It had been her dream ever since she was seven years old, and now she was doing it at twenty-seven. She tore the envelope open and grinned —the number was higher than it had been last month. She was getting paid well for her drawing.

Last year, after a few missteps and a lot of chickening out, she had walked into the office of the publishers Abbott & Merchant and had blown them away. Or so they said three months later when they offered to buy all nine of the children's books she had completed.

The last envelope was even more important than the paycheck but wouldn't be possible without the paycheck. It was a letter from her lawyer, not the lawyer it should be, but a stranger instead. Just as she was getting published, her stepmom married a lawyer, but by then, she was already with someone else. Opening it, she saw the papers Aspen Andrews had told her she was sending on Friday. In two weeks, she would own the house behind her, every inch of it. Not that she had been worried that the current owner would kick her out since it was her dad. But she wanted to own it and not have to think about the future. It would be hers.

So far, she hadn't told Sera or any of her sisters that she was buying the house from their father because then she would have to tell them that she had quit her job as a bartender at various clubs and bars around town. Then she'd also have to tell them that she didn't actually need the job at her sisters' catering company anymore either. She hadn't told them that she had sold her books.

Yes, she should tell them, but it just never came up. Agatha was known as the unpredictable one, the jobless one, the one who was home and dependable. Sure, being unpredictable and dependable usually didn't happen at the same time—she hadn't been unpredictable for a few years now, but the memory still lingered with her family.

As she waited, she noticed the for sale sign was gone from the front yard of the big old house across the street. Hilda Jenkins had lived there for over sixty years, but she was gone now. In all her twenty-seven years, Agatha hadn't made it past the front door of any of the houses on the block. The closest she had gotten was during trick or treating. Never had one of her few friends lived on her street. Sera and Harrison had recently bought a nice house two blocks over, and that was the only one she had been in on that block. Agatha had always dreamed of having a friend right next door, but that had never happened, much to her disappointment.

When she had been growing up, all the houses in her neighborhood contained old people—at least, maybe they seemed old only because she was a kid. But since they were only now dying off, they were possibly not as old as Agatha had thought back then. Now there were families and kids and block parties; the street was far more active than it had ever been before. So far, she couldn't say if she liked it or not.

Agatha grinned when she caught sight of the little dark-haired girl with the pink backpack of a cartoon character that Agatha could now discuss ad nauseam because Violet had told her all about it. The kid wasn't Sera's baby for nothing. Bubbly and an extrovert with a capital E, Violet was always happy and always talking, even before Agatha could hear her.

Today Violet turned nine. She was getting older and would soon lose interest in her boring, quiet older sister, but for now, the kid loved Agatha and would spend every day with her if possible. She usually spent two hours with Violet before her parents came home from work. It wasn't the time she had spent with older sister Emma when she was this age, but it was something.

Agatha had been eleven when Emma was born to her new step-mom, her dad already gone. Agatha had only needed one look at the baby to know that they were sisters; they both had the same fine black hair. Though the two shared no blood, they were bonded from the beginning. Agatha took an active role in raising the baby and had been her primary babysitter. Her other sisters were busy with school activities, which Agatha had no interest in. At the time when it should have bothered her that she had to stay home, she had actually loved having a built-in excuse.

When Agatha was nineteen, Sera had brought home Violet, another black-haired baby for Agatha to love. That time around, Agatha didn't have to work around school, as it had only taken her a few weeks to know that art school was not for her. She just wanted to do what she wanted to do, no assignments. So, she had been sort of a nanny for years and worked nights as a bartender, but she had been able to spend her days with her baby sisters. Now that they were older, she missed those times.

"Emma got to go home and said I could not," was all Agatha heard Violet say as the girl walked past the mailbox and started up the steps.

"Because you have to stay away until your party," Agatha explained yet again. They had talked about Violet's party a dozen times since the plan had been hatched, each time the younger girl arguing why the plan was bad.

"But I want the party now." The little girl stomped her foot before heading up the steps to Agatha.

"You'll just have to wait," Agatha said firmly. Sera wouldn't like it if she brought her daughter home now. She and Harrison had taken the day off to get ready for the party. Agatha knew that they had done other things besides getting ready for the party because a kid-free day was a kid-free day.

"Can I open the present from you?" A little black eyebrow went up, and Violet's blue eyes stared at her in question.

"I promised to bring it to the party." Agatha accepted Violet's ready hug.

"Please, Ag!" she begged.

"Can you act surprised when you open it again?" Agatha laughed. She couldn't say no to her.

"Of course I can." She knew the girl couldn't; she was the worst secret-keeper in the family.

"You must be the Cramers," came a voice from the bottom of the stairs. "I'm Chris Lowell. I just bought the Jenkins house."

Peeking out from behind Violet, Agatha suddenly couldn't breathe. *Chris Lowell?* She hadn't seen him in almost two years. She assumed he was still a big football star, so why was he buying a house in her neighborhood? In her safe, little Chris-free neighborhood.

Looking him over, Agatha noticed that his curls were back and that he wasn't as broad as he was before. He still had some amazing muscles in his arms, but not like that night two years ago.

Even then, she knew sleeping with Chris was a mistake, and doing it the night before an important career-changing meeting was her worst mistake. She missed her meeting and everything that it could have brought into her life. All because she spent the night with him when she knew she shouldn't.

His eyes were looking her over from head to toe. She wondered if he would recognize her this time. He had last time, but she had changed since then—changed a lot. Two years before, she had been stick-skinny with crazy hair. Since then, she had gained forty pounds. The mohawk had grown into a black bob that was now just above her shoulders, though still stick-straight because Agatha had never had curls. She looked a lot like a mom and less like a homeless druggie, even if she didn't have kids of her own.

"No, the Cramers live there." Violet pointed at the house next door. "I am Violet, and this is Agatha. We live here. Sorry, I mean I live down there, and she lives here now."

Agatha couldn't stand another moment near him. After all, nothing had changed in two years or even since high school. "Violet, I'm sure he's not interested." Her body wanted him to remember her even though her heart begged him not to. Agatha needed walls between them. She couldn't do this today; today was Violet's birthday. She needed to focus on her.

"Agatha? I pictured someone a lot older." Chris's brown eyes were still as captivating as they had been at thirteen when he called her Chrissy all year, and as panty-melting as they had been in that hotel room at twenty-five.

"Sorry, just me with an old lady name." She shrugged and took Violet's hand. "We have to have a snack. See you around the neighborhood."

No way was she sticking around in case he actually realized who she was. If that ever happened, he seemed to have the ability to forget her. She wished she had that ability.

"See you around," he called.

Agatha took her sister into her house to feed her and let her open the present..

CHAPTER SIX

THE PLUMBING WAS COMPLETELY SHOT. It had gone unnoticed during the inspection and during the last week since Chris had moved into the big old house. The entire kitchen had been flooded this morning when he woke up, and he realized just how bad it was.

It had taken all morning to get the water cleaned up, and now he was without running water to the kitchen until he could figure out how to run new pipes or hire someone to do it. He was starting to think that hiring it out was the better choice when it came to plumbing.

After the water was cleaned up, he went back to scraping the paint off the wainscoting from the woodwork in the downstairs bathroom. Chris figured it would probably take the rest of his natural life.

He was taking a break on his porch when he saw her. She was sitting on her front step, reading her mail. The picture of the perfect mom waiting for her kids to come home. Her dark hair was in a style that framed her face and made her run her fingers through it regularly to keep it out of her eyes. She seemed familiar, but he couldn't place where he knew her from. She was wearing blue jeans and a red shirt. As he watched her, he couldn't stop himself from going to talk to her, to see who she was. Based on what he had seen of the neighborhood this last week, she was probably married with a ton of kids.

He was almost to her house when a kid who looked just like her had bounced down the sidewalk and gave her a hug. But he was already there, so he decided to introduce himself and be a good neighbor anyway. As he drew close enough, he saw her shirt said "Habby B=Dya," and couldn't figure out the meaning behind it.

She hadn't been the friendliest of neighbors, and if it hadn't been for the kid, she probably would have ignored him completely. Everything from her tone to her posture said he was bothering her. Well, he didn't need her. He had a house to continue working on, and he didn't need distractions from that.

Back across the street, he decided against working on the wainscoting and instead focused on watching a video on how to change out light fixtures. The ones that had been in the house for too many decades were atrocious and needed to be gone. Soon.

Settling himself on his porch step like his neighbor had, he scrolled through his phone looking for a good video. After watching six, he knew exactly what he was doing and decided to head to the store to buy what he would need.

Before he got up, Agatha from across the street walked out of her house with the little girl right next to her, carrying a brightly wrapped package.

He didn't know why he was so drawn to her. There was just something about her that made him want to walk across the street to talk to her again. But based on her coldness toward him earlier, he decided to stay away.

It wasn't like he was attracted to Agatha; he had never been attracted to women like her. The woman he had been seeing when he had blown out his knee was the type of woman he liked: tall, blonde, and beautiful. Tara had been a model and had been devoted to him. At least until his career had ended. Then she had left him.

He had been in the hospital when she left. She hadn't even told him it was over; she just found someone else. It hadn't even bothered him that she had left. From the beginning of their relationship, they had been different. He had been interested in his career, and she had been interested in what his career would do for her.

Looking back, he wished he hadn't even dated her, except she was exactly the type of women he had always dated: self-centered and beautiful.

He had been drawn to women who wanted something from him, and for years, he had been happy to give it in exchange for others to envy him for who was on his arm. For a time, it had been worth it. Not so much anymore.

Watching Agatha and Violet walk down the street, he could tell the girl was talking as they went. Agatha was silently walking beside her, letting her chatter away.

Chris got into his truck and tried not to watch them in the mirror. He tried not to focus on Agatha's hips swaying in her blue-jeans but failed.

CHAPTER SEVEN

THE HOUSE WAS PACKED, and yet still more people continued to arrive. When Sera had walked her through the house months before, Agatha had thought that it was roomy and spacious. Not anymore. Now it was crowded and loud. It didn't help that Harrison and Jonas were fighting with each other over something. She didn't even care what it was about; they were just loud.

"If you're just going to argue, go out on the deck," Harper told the pair from the kitchen in frustration. And she wasn't even married to one of them.

Sera, with a baby in her arms, pushed her husband outside. "So you don't wake the babies." Lucy and Leo had twin boys who were a couple months old, and if Sera was in a room with them, she was carrying one. Agatha didn't know what was going to happen when she had her own baby in a month.

"I'll join them," Kaine said after kissing his wife on the cheek as he walked by. Harper even stopped for a moment and let him do it. Then she turned her attention back to cutting buns, busy as ever.

"How are Louisa and Frankie?" Lucy asked Buzz as she mixed a dip.

Louisa and Frankie were not only Buzz's husband, Jonas's, half-sisters, but also half-sisters to the Lovely sisters. Buzz had found that out when she had accidentally-on-purpose worked a week for the woman who had given them life. In that time, she had fallen for Jonas and met and befriended the sisters. Though so far, they were only in contact with Buzz and Jonas.

"Good, in Chicago still. We had hoped that Louisa would start school here, but Frankie got a job there, so they're staying put. I like that they're together, but I wish they were here. Jonas found them a great apartment, so they at least have that. I wish I had that apartment when I was single," Buzz said from the couch as she tried to adjust the sleeping baby in her arms around her own protruding stomach. She had over a month left on her pregnancy, but Buzz Raiden was done with it. So far, she had not taken to pregnancy, and it seemed holding babies was now defeating her as well.

She set Luke down on the couch between herself and Agatha, not wanting to give him over to anyone but unable to hold him.

"Tell them hi next time, Buzz," Sera said, sitting down with Owen still in her arms, her belly not getting in her way. Fifteen years ago, she had chosen to raise five girls that she didn't have to, and now she was willing to take on more by trying to take Louisa and Frankie under her wing. Though the women, both over twenty, weren't looking for a new mom, Sera still tried.

Agatha looked at the bald baby beside her. He looked just like his twin brother. They were a few months old, and their mother was already tossing them aside to make some fancy meal for Violet's birthday. Not that her sister didn't love the babies, but cooking was her first love.

"Sit down, Lucy, you just had babies. What can I do?" Agatha pushed herself away from the couch and away from the babies.

"No, Ag. It is mostly ready," Harper answered for her sister and business partner. For a couple of months now, she had been trying to let Lucy do more, but talking didn't seem to be one of those things today.

Ignoring her oldest sister, Agatha grabbed Lucy's hand and pulled her from the kitchen. "Stop, Lucy. Sit down."

Sighing, Lucy let Agatha pull her away from her favorite room. Sitting on the couch where Agatha had been, Lucy touched her son's head and then picked him up and hugged him to her.

Smiling at the scene, Agatha pushed from her mind how close Lucy had come to putting the boys up for adoption. At the time, she thought that she couldn't be a good mom and would put them in danger. It had taken the entire family and her now-husband to talk her down from that ledge. Agatha couldn't see her as anything but a mommy now.

Lucy looked up from her baby and said, "So Sera, only a month to go."

"I had forgotten how bad the last month was," Sera replied, but she didn't sound like it was bad. Sera was always upbeat. "I can't believe it's a boy this time!"

"We're waiting to find out," Buzz said, looking up. The redhead was also due in a little over a month, and Agatha hoped that she would have a redhead. Even though she had gotten C's in science, she knew that thanks to her dark-haired husband, that might not happen.

"So, Harper, when are you and Kaine going to start trying to have kids?" Sera asked.

"They haven't been married that long, Sera," Buzz answered for her even though the couple had been married for months longer than Buzz herself.

"Why do pregnant people always want more people to get pregnant?" Agatha asked. Her eyes strayed to the kitchen where Harper was busily ignoring the conversation. Lately when asked, Harper didn't have the snarky comments about babies she usually did.

"Because we love to share the misery," Buzz answered with a laugh.

"It's 6 p.m. I better get the meal going so Violet won't say I wrecked her birthday," Harper said from the kitchen.

Buzz shimmied off the couch. "I'll help." Buzz shared Agatha's shortness, which made pregnancy miserable for her baby sister.

"Me too." Lucy jumped up and handed the baby she was holding to Agatha.

With the baby now in her arms, Agatha sat down where Buzz had been and pulled her legs under her and looked at the baby. He was so different than how Violet and Emma had been. They had hair when they were born.

Sera changed seats to sit next to her, which made Agatha smile. "It's different than the girls, right?"

"Different, so much could've been different." Sera's voice was shaky.

Agatha turned to her and saw tears in her eyes. Quietly she hissed, "Don't."

"Sorry, just too many hormones. Nine years today, Ag." Sera let the tears fall.

"Stop it, Mom. It happened for a reason. It turned out for the best." Agatha put her arm around her mom. It was odd that she was comforting the other woman today.

"But it still hurts, Ag. I know you still think about it. Wonder what could have been," Sera said.

"Not every day, not anymore," Agatha admitted and stood up before she started crying too.

Carrying the baby into the kitchen, she handed him over to Maby, who had just arrived. As the group chatted, she excused herself to the bathroom on the first floor. Closing the door behind her, she let the tears fall, not for the first time that day.

Today, she had to see Chris today of all days: Violet's ninth birthday. He showed up on her front step nine years too late. What would he have found if he had been there nine years earlier, when she had needed him?

The evening Violet had been born, Sera and Agatha had already been at the hospital all day. Since 2 a.m. actually, because that was the time Agatha had woken up to bad cramps. Sera had rushed her to the hospital. She had no idea what was happening or why Agatha was in pain. By midmorning, Agatha had lost the baby she had been carrying for four months, Chris's baby. A baby she had been hiding from her family, not knowing how to tell anyone about. All the excitement caused Sera to go into labor, and by evening, Violet had been born.

Violet was only two weeks early, and Sera's delivery had been quick and had made Agatha's pain of losing her own baby lighter.

Sera had let Agatha name the tiny girl Violet because Agatha had been in a deep purple mood that evening. Hours before, she had named her lost baby Jet, to match her own black mood. Her sisters had never known about her baby, and Sera had promised not to tell. So far, she had kept that promise. There were just some things she didn't want to share with everyone.

In the weeks following the births, the two had become closer than before. Since only Buzz was living at home still, it had been easy not to tell everyone about Agatha's issues. Sera just told everyone she was sick. No details were given, and nobody asked for more.

With them both at home recovering, they bonded over each's situation and the baby they both could love. Sera had told her who the father was and that he was also Emma's father. Agatha had told her some of her obsession with Christopher, but not all. It had still been too painful then.

What she would have done with her own child all these years, Agatha didn't know. She knew her sisters would have loved him and helped with his care, and Agatha wouldn't have been able to let her life slide for years without any ambition or motivation. But deep down, she knew she wasn't mom material. Sure, she was good with kids and loved them, but *being* a mom was different. She had always felt she was more like her own mother, who had walked away from her own children before Agatha was even in school.

She had told Sera she didn't think of the baby everyday anymore, and she didn't. But some days, she could almost see him. It had been a boy; even if the doctor wouldn't say, Agatha knew. Today was one of those days she had seen him walking with Violet from the bus. Jet. Blond hair and brown eyes. He was not bubbly and talkative but let Violet talk for him. He always had.

Washing her face with cold water, she pushed the memory of what could have been down deep and went out to celebrate her baby sister's birthday. It was a special day for her. Agatha had always made sure that there was no sadness on this day.

By the time she made it out of the bathroom, people had started to eat. Nobody noticed when she came into the room, which she was happy for because she didn't know how long she had been gone.

"Nice shirt, Agatha," Lucy said, rolling her eyes.

Agatha loved her shirt. It was her go-to birthday shirt. Years ago, Lucy had started a screen-printing business. It had been short-lived but had supplied the family with shirts until the end of time because they had kept the rejects. Habby B=dya should have read Happy B-day, and the large quantity of mistakes should have been a sign to everyone that something was wrong with the twin, but at the time, they had laughed it off and teased Lucy about it. But last year, Cliff had realized that she had undiagnosed dyslexia, and she wasn't as ditzy as she let everyone believe.

"I love this one," Agatha argued. "And the one that says 'Pins.' And, of course, 'Grand Cannon,' but we all have that one."

"We should all go to the Grand Canyon and wear our Grand Cannon shirts," Maby said with a laugh as she dished up a salad.

"How many 'Cuymun Islunb's' do we have? I like that one." Sera chuckled.

"Not enough for a vacation," Lucy grumbled. Talk about the shirts always made Lucy self-conscious because they reminded her of her disability.

"We are not making fun of you, Lucy. I love the shirts. People stop and ask where I got my shirt. They're funny," Maby reassured her twin.

"I think if you still have the stuff, you should make all the girls a shirt that says their long name, the entire thing," Leo said, kissing a frowning Lucy on the neck.

"Oh, now you're bringing out the long name," Maby replied in her teacher voice.

Leo laughed. "Yes, I am. And I would proudly wear Lucy Maude's name on my chest."

Each of the five older sisters had a hideously long name. Most had been named after authors, including Agatha Christie Lovely, Nelle Harper Lee Lovely, Lucy Maud Montgomery Lovely, and Beatrix Potter

Lovely, known as Buzz. Only Mabel Lucie Attwell Lovely had been named for an illustrator, but Buzz's namesake technically was one too.

So, using someone's long name meant business in this house. Maby and Lucy had the longest, and when they came out, that meant the twins were really fighting.

"How about just the portrait of the person we're named after? Then nobody would really know who they were," Agatha suggested, her mood brightening.

"We should!" Lucy nodded enthusiastically.

"We shouldn't," Buzz said, stabbing at her salad.

"Really, Buzz? Agatha is on board but not you?" Maby said, and all eyes turned to the redhead.

"I'm not feeling up for anything right now." Buzz was not Buzz when she was miserably pregnant.

"Maybe next summer," Maby replied. Then added, "Has anyone seen the star of Harry Truman High School?"

"Who?" Lucy asked.

"Christopher Lowell. He's back and bought a place on this street. Don't know which one exactly." Where Maby got her information, Agatha had no idea.

"Are you still hung up on him? Aren't you married?" Harper said.

"I am not hung up on him; I just hear things," she said in defense.

Agatha chuckled at her sister. She had always wanted to be one of the popular kids in high school, making a point of knowing what was happening at school.

"Who is this guy trying to steal my woman?" Cliff said, pulling his wife closer to him.

"Football star. You can't compete with him, Cliff," Lucy answered, teasing her friend. They had been best friends before Cliff fell for Maby.

"I'll fight him to the death," Cliff told the room and pretended to bite Maby on the neck? Either way, it made her giggle.

Lucy laughed. "He would have no idea why you're poking him with your weak little arms, Cliff. He had no idea who Maby was in high school. We didn't run in the same circles."

"I think he bought Hilda's house. It's been for sale for a while," Sera said, moving the conversation away from Cliff's wife.

Around a mouthful of BBQ, Violet said, "We met the new neighbor after school. He was a big, tall guy."

"Is it him, Agatha?" Sera asked. Sera was the only one who knew anything about her infatuation with Chris.

"I think so, but it's hard to tell. He's changed since I last saw him." Agatha shrugged.

"He looked pretty good at that press thing we catered a few years ago. Were you there, Agatha?" Lucy asked.

"I don't remember," Agatha lied.

Every moment had been seared into her memory.

"Then you must not have been there, wow," Buzz said and was rewarded by Jonas sliding his hand over her mouth and whispering in her ear, making her blush.

"That's not really my type anyway. I'm not into sports guys." Agatha grabbed a plate and started to fill it since everyone else had already been through the line.

"I have a friend I think you would like," Jonas said from the table.

"He is pretty cute," Buzz added and pulled her head from her husband's hand before he could cover her mouth.

"I know a guy at the college who would love you," Maby said, getting into the matching game.

"Me?" Agatha questioned, leaning against the wall to eat since the table was packed. "I don't need to be loved."

"And then she makes me cry," Sera said as tears rolled down her cheeks.

Harrison rushed to put an arm around his wife and pointed his fork at Agatha. "Tell your mother you need love, Agatha. You made her cry."

"Sorry, Mom. Didn't think it would make you cry," Agatha said, regretting saying the words out loud, even if she believed them completely.

"It's just the day, the hormones," Sera said, and Agatha stiffened at her words. But by then, conversation had started around the table again, mostly about Agatha and her dating life, filling in the new men in the family to what life was like in a house full of adult women. Agatha made sure that they each knew that their new loves were not as innocent as they pretended to be.

One story led to another, and before long, Agatha wasn't even being mentioned anymore. Looking around the table, she was happy for each of her sisters and their mother; they all deserved to be as happy as they were. Not her, though. She made her own happiness, and soon she would own her house and finish her latest book. They might have needed a man to be happy, but not her.

CHAPTER EIGHT

In his attempt to fix the plaster in the master bedroom, the entire ceiling had fallen on his head. Okay, it was only all the plaster from the ceiling, but it was now all on the floor. Chris wasn't hurt, just extremely dusty.

It had been a full week in the house, and so far, nothing had gone right. Nothing that was on his list was done or even started. He had no water in the kitchen, and the floors hadn't survived their Monday bath and were now buckling. The upstairs bathroom was also unusable due to a toilet that wouldn't stop running. He'd started to work with it, and now it wouldn't run at all. He had no idea how you even killed a toilet, but he had, which made him scared to do anything with the other bathroom. Now the ceiling of his bedroom was on the floor, and the sudden crash had made the ceiling in the dining room do the same thing.

Shaking his head, he pulled off his T-shirt and tossed it into the destroyed dining room. Heading out the door, he turned on the hose and rinsed the dust from his hair and face. Chris tossed the hose down, turned off the water, and saw her sitting on her front step, watching him.

When he looked at her, she didn't even avert her eyes, just stared.

Agatha. He still couldn't believe that was her name. So far, he had seen her every day since they had met. Mostly because he realized on Tuesday that she went and waited for the little girl to come to her house. Sometimes a bigger girl would come too, and Agatha always waited outside for them.

Since she was sitting there, it must be after 3:00 p.m. but before 3:20; she was only there a narrow window of time. So far, he hadn't noticed a man hanging out near the house. A pregnant blonde would come and walk the girl away after 5:00 p.m., heading in the same direction as Agatha had gone the first day they had met. It seemed that Agatha was only the babysitter.

Since she was still staring, he waved. She waved back and then smiled, but not to him. She had turned to the little girl walking up the street alone today. He couldn't hear what they said, but they chatted about something, then the little girl sat down next to Agatha and waved at him.

Waving again, he headed across the street. Neither moved, though to be honest, he was watching Agatha more than the little girl. Today, Agatha's gray shirt said "Cancan" across her breasts, very nice breasts.

"Hi, Violet." He ignored the black-haired woman and ran his fingers through his still-wet hair, realizing that he had gotten his jeans a little wet also. But there was nothing he could do about it now.

"Hi! Are you fixing the house over there? My mom and dad bought a house but had to do so much to it. But now it's done, and Dad can relax. Or so he says. Mom says he'll get bored." The girl seemed to give way more information than was needed.

"Do you think he'll get bored?" Chris asked, leaning against the railing of the bottom step, something he would never do at his place because his porch was falling apart. Or it was now that he had tried to fix some of the railings earlier in the day.

Violet shrugged. "No, he didn't really like to fix the house. He just did it for Mom."

"I bet your mom is worth it," he said. All moms are great when you're young.

"She's okay. You're not wearing a shirt. The rule at my house is you have to wear a shirt, even Mom and Dad." The kid looked him up and down with slight disappointment that he would break a rule.

"I just got dust all over mine, and the rest need to be washed." He shrugged. His weekend plans included a visit to the laundromat. If Agatha wasn't going to talk to him, he could talk to the girl; she wanted to talk.

"What size are you?" Violet asked.

"Extra large." He looked at her blue eyes, different from her babysitter's brown ones. Also different because Agatha's were full of judgment. He would not be winning any cases in front of her.

Violet leaned toward him. "What's your favorite color?"

"Blue." He grinned at her random questions.

"Okay." She jumped up and ran into the house, leaving him alone with a silent Agatha.

"What is Cancan?" he asked, looking at her shirt, or breasts, or both.

"The cancan is a dance. It's a misspelling of Cancun. My sister made it a few years ago. She has dyslexia," she explained, looking down at her shirt and pulling it out a little so she could see the letters.

"Why do you wear it if it's spelled wrong?" He liked that she was finally giving him the time of day He was liking the quirky personality he was discovering. He was liking her.

She shrugged. "Because it's more fun this way, and they're free."

The kid ran out of the house holding a blue shirt that she handed to him with a smile. Pulling it on, it he looked down to see it said "Basten."

"What should it say?"

"Boston, I think. Lucy might know, but I've never picked up on her spellings," Agatha said, standing up with her mail in her hand. "Time for a snack, Violet."

"Bye! You can keep the shirt; we have more," Violet said and followed Agatha into the house, blocking Chris's view of her backside.

Once the door shut, he headed back to his place and wondered what to do now. The house was falling apart a little more every day.

He was failing for the first time in his life, and it made him uneasy, but something was making him stick to it.

CHAPTER NINE

Hanging up her phone, Agatha headed away from her drawing to find the serving dish Harper had described to her over the phone. Most of Harper's stuff had been moved to her new place months before, when her husband, Kaine, had remodeled his kitchen into a commercial kitchen for her.

But it seemed there was still a pile of serving platters she'd left at the house that she needed next week for a big event. Agatha would no doubt be roped into helping out, but now that she was only helping out a day or two a week, she was okay with it. When she had worked an event nearly every night, she hadn't been. Or when she had to hold down a job. Then add working for her sisters, and it got to be a lot.

Agatha turned on all the lights as she went through the house. It was a little spooky to be there alone, so sometimes she just pretended one of her sisters was in their room so that she wasn't alone. In the kitchen, she dug out the pile of platters from the pantry, still mostly full of Lucy and Harper's stuff. It was from this pantry that they produced their breakfast meals when they came over. Agatha didn't go into it when they weren't around. Since they usually dropped off leftovers when they came, she didn't need anything from the pantry. What little food she had in the house was in a cabinet, leaving the pantry as storage for her sisters. She carried the platters to the table by the front door so that they could be grabbed if Harper had no time to talk or Agatha was sleeping when she stopped by.

The neighborhood was dark at two in the morning. She was the only mouse stirring that night. Setting the platter down by the front door, she nearly screamed when there was a sudden knock. Hand on heart, she looked out the side window and saw a large form standing on her front step. It knocked again as she watched. When the person ran a hand through his hair, she recognized the movement: Chris.

Chris, who had so far not recognized her at all. Either he had not remembered her from high school and had been so drunk eighteen months before, or she had changed that much over the years. Or maybe it was a combination of both.

Eighteen months ago, he hadn't remembered who she was the morning after. She had realized that right away when she was hunting for her clothes. His knowing her was lost to the booze he had consumed. Sober, he hadn't remembered her. He probably didn't even remember their night of sex. Hot, wild sex that she couldn't get out of her mind even all these months later.

Agatha slowly opened the door for him, secretly hoping he wanted to fuck her again. Over and over again.

"Hey, Agatha, I saw your light on. Could I borrow a flashlight? I'll bring it right back," he said with relief.

"Don't you have a flashlight?" She leaned against the edge of the door, trying not to throw herself in his arms.

"No, I don't. Nor do I have any lights in my house right now." She could tell he was trying to hide his frustration.

"Hold on a minute," she said and left him alone in the open doorway.

Finding the flashlights in the stairwell to the basement, she took two and headed back to Chris. She hoped she was only horny for him because she hadn't gotten any in a while, not because she was back on Team Chris. She was too old and smart to join that team again.

"I brought two in case the batteries are low in one. What happened to your electricity?" She walked toward him. He had let himself in and was looking around the living room. His hands were stuffed in his jeans, and he was wearing a gray sweatshirt that hid all those awesome muscles.

He reached for one of the flashlights. "I don't know. I was putting in a new light fixture and poof—all the lights went out."

"Did the wires touch?" she asked, still holding the other flashlight.

"No," he answered quickly, then added, "Maybe."

"Do you have fuses or breakers?" She folded her arms, deciding that maybe he shouldn't be dealing with electricity.

"Yes," he answered and looked around the living room again.

"Do you have any idea what you are doing?" She pushed past him and headed over to his house.

He was close on her heels but let her lead. He was over a foot taller than her and an athlete. Agatha knew he could have carried her faster than she could walk over there.

"I have some idea," he said as she opened the door on the old house.

"Where was the light?" she demanded as she turned on her flashlight.

Behind her, he turned on his as well and pointed it the center of the room. A ladder stood under a little black hole in the ceiling. Agatha climbed up the ladder and looked at the hole. She tried to ignore that Chris was watching her every move, that he was very close to her, too close for her liking.

Realizing that the wires *were* touching, she knew what had happened. She climbed down the ladder and went back to her house to grab the tools she needed. She knew better to ask him for anything; he didn't even have a flashlight.

Chris was still standing in the middle of the floor with his flashlight beam on the hole when she returned. Climbing the ladder again, she put the caps on each of the wires and turned to him. With her on the ladder, she was taller than him for once, and she liked it. She enjoyed seeing his face turned up and looking at her, or the hole, it didn't matter.

"Fuse box?" she asked as she climbed down.

"Basement."

Chris grabbed Agatha around the waist and lifted her to the ground as if she weighed nothing from her perch on the third rung. His hands lingered for a moment too long until Agatha pulled away from him. No need to give him the idea that she was interested; she was smarter than that now.

He led her to the kitchen and then down the stairs to the basement, which was as dark as the rest of the house. Agatha hated basements; they were dark and smelly, and all the spiders lived there.

He pointed to the box on the wall. "Here."

Agatha looked at it for a moment and flipped the biggest of the switches. The lights blazed on around them, and the hum of electronics and appliances filled the silence.

"Fixed." She grinned at him. "But you have got to stop touching anything that you don't know how to fix."

"How am I going to learn if I don't try?" His brown eyes were on her.

"Not by burning down your house, because that's what would have happened if the circuit breaker hadn't switched. Fire, Chris." She folded her arms.

"How did you learn?"

"My mom taught me. I don't know if she wants to teach you," Agatha said. Sera had taught them all the basics for house and lawn care. She had single-mom'd like a pro.

"Maybe *you* could teach me." He shot his killer grin at her.

Agatha pushed past him. His flirting reminding her of everything that had come before today, but his charm wasn't going to work on her again. She was over Chris Lowell, had been for years.

"I don't think so." She headed back up the stairs to the brightly lit kitchen and stopped in her tracks. "Was it like this when you bought it? Did Hilda live like this?"

The floorboards were twisted and separating from each other. Many of the cabinet doors were gone, and the fridge was in the middle of the room. There was no stove, and the sink was full and overflowing with Styrofoam food containers and pop cans and bottles.

"No, I was working and had some issues," he admitted from behind her.

"Holy fuck, do you have any idea what you are doing?" she questioned and walked through the kitchen into the dining room that was full of small bits of plaster.

"I'm learning, Agatha!" he said angrily.

Covering her mouth with her hand, she replied, "Have you had this checked for asbestos?"

"I never thought of that."

"And lead, because there is lead for sure. It's an old house." Agatha couldn't believe what she was seeing. He had only been here a week.

"No, I haven't," he admitted and ran his fingers through his hair.

She turned to him. "You should. You're not living here, are you?"

"Yup, there are five bedrooms." He shrugged as if the mess wouldn't kill him.

"I think you should find another place to live." She suggested looking around the place and wondered if his bedroom was in just as bad of shape as the rest of the house.

"I guess I could get a hotel." He said the words, but there wasn't any conviction behind them.

Agatha knew it was late, and by the time he got a hotel room, it would be morning. But she also had empty rooms, a lot of them. Though she hated being a good person, she was.

On a sigh, she said, "Get your stuff. You can stay with me tonight. You're just lucky I have empty rooms, and I think you might kill yourself if you're left alone."

"Hey! I have yet to kill myself," he said and folded his arms and grinned at her, not saying whether he was taking her up on her offer or not.

"'Yet' is the key word. Get your stuff and come over; I'll make up a bedroom," she said again and took the flashlight from his hand. She didn't want to lose them in case he never came over.

Walking out of his house, she wondered what she was doing by letting him stay with her. Really? Christopher Lowell! She was a moron, and she knew it.

CHAPTER TEN

WAS his entire house really full of carcinogens? Looking around the two rooms that were complete disasters, he wondered if Agatha was right that his house would kill him one day. Now or in the future.

He wondered if she would be willing to help him fix the house since he wasn't doing so great at it. Then he could spend his days watching her ass as she sashayed around, being an expert on everything. Today's green shirt said "Hlltam Hoob" in bright pink. Her black hair had been the same as it was almost twelve hours before, just a bit messier.

When his lights had gone out, and he had seen that hers were on, he went over to borrow a flashlight—another item to add to his list of things needed for the house. That list was so long. Not that he had thought she would actually answer the door because it was two in the morning, and he was practically a stranger.

Once she had opened the door, he had learned something completely new about the woman. Agatha was small, smaller than he had thought she was sitting on her front step. She was maybe just over five feet tall, and that was with her orange tennis shoes on. Since he was 6'5", she was tiny compared to him, tiny and light. He had noticed when he had lifted her off the ladder. He grabbed a few things upstairs and turned off the lights as he left the house. She may be a stranger, but her house wasn't trying to kill him. Until he got things checked out at his place, he was homeless. Tomorrow he would have to find a place to live for a while. Tonight, he was happy he would be staying across the street even if Agatha didn't seem exactly happy about the idea. She had offered, and he had taken her up on it. Not only was he getting a place to stay, but he would get to spend time with her.

When Chris made it to Agatha's door, he wondered if he should knock. She had invited him, but did that mean he should just barge in? He decided it must, so he walked into her brightly lit house. He had noticed the comfortable furniture before when she got the flashlights. There were two couches and a loveseat in tan with bright colored throw pillows, which contrasted with the walls that were a bright yellow, and the ceiling was even brighter yellow.

Chris didn't see Agatha, but he could hear her upstairs, so he headed up to find her. On the top floor, he realized that her house must be bigger than his because there were eight bedroom doors visible. Hearing her in one at the far end of the hall, he followed the noise and found her throwing a light blue comforter on the top of the bed, which matched the paler blue of the walls. Leaning against the door, he watched her. He could tell she had not been ready for company.

"Sorry to put you out like this. I could get a hotel for the night." He stood, holding his stuff, hoping she didn't send him away.

"No, I just have to change the sheets. I don't remember who was the last in here or even when." She tossed a pillow back on the bed that she had put on the dresser.

"So long ago?" he asked.

"Not too long. Maybe a few months. But who was it and why?" She bit her lip as she thought about it.

"Best to change the sheets then." He grinned.

"Oh yeah, sheets needed to be changed," she said, not looking at him.

Chris walked in and set his stuff on the dresser. "Whose room was it?"

"Mabel, but she moved in with her boyfriend—sorry, husband now, Cliff."

"Mabel and Cliff? Was he a soldier fighting in the great war?" he teased.

She laughed at his joke. "I wish. His name is Clifton Scott V. Yes, those Scotts, and she had shit parents."

"I don't recall any Scotts," he said, racking his brain for who they could be. Probably someone important. His dad probably knew them.

"Old money. I'm sure you heard about the new library. They're putting up half the money." She shrugged as she stuffed the pillow into a case.

He let out a whistle. "Mabel married well."

"*Cliff* married well. He got Maby." She turned to him. "Bathroom is down the hallway, and sleep as late as you want."

"See you at the bathroom, roomie." He watched her walk out the door.

"Nope, I have my own," she said as she left. He followed to see what door she went in. It was one closest to the stairs and farthest from his bedroom. He wondered if that was why she had chosen this room for him.

Looking around him, he saw no cracked or falling plaster. Everything looked neat and tidy and lived in. Even though the house was basically empty, it was still clean and tidy.

Chris probably spent too long in the working shower, but he was just glad he didn't wreck anything while he was in there. The room was well-organized and stocked with anything imaginable one might need. Or anything if you were a woman, because there was nothing but girly stuff everywhere. Since it was there, he used the body wash and shampoo and ended up smelling like a field of flowers. Like Agatha.

After crawling into bed, he wondered about the woman of the house. Tonight, she had been less prickly than she had been before. At first, he didn't think she would give him a flashlight, much less a bed, though he had to admit he would rather be in her bed for the night.

CHAPTER ELEVEN

FILLING in the brown of the donkey's butt, Agatha felt someone watching her. Hoping it was not her houseguest, but also hoping it was not one of her sisters, she looked up into the blue eyes of Violet. Pulling off her headphone, she smiled at the little girl.

"I brought you muffins!" Violet held up a plate so that Agatha could see them.

"Thank you, Violet. You are the nicest person I know." Agatha set her brown pencil down and got up to hug her.

"Mom said you would be sleeping in your room, but you were not. I knew you would be up here," Violet chatted as Agatha took the plate from her.

"Let's go see Mom. Is anyone else here?" Agatha knew the answer had to be yes. There were muffins, and Sera did not cook breakfast.

Violet scurried down the stairs, and Agatha followed more slowly, not in quite the same hurry to see who had shown up. On the second floor, she saw that Maby's bedroom door was still closed, which meant he was still there. Yes, she had let that man stay with her, but only for one night. Tonight, he would have to stay somewhere else. Anywhere else.

After leaving him to shower, she'd tried not to listen to the shower running in the quiet house until she had given up on sleep. Her mind was just replaying that night eighteen months ago, and her body was getting all worked up.

When she'd gotten out of bed, she didn't know if she should join him in the shower or go for a run. She hadn't run since high school, and they had forced her to do that, so she made herself go up to her studio, a new name for the room, and work. Getting lost in her work always took her mind off life.

But he was still there, and so were three of her sisters and her mom. Not counting Violet.

"Violet said you were drawing. This late?" Harper asked as she slid a pan into the oven.

"Time got away from me," she admitted. She had planned to sleep last night. Now she would when her family left.

"Have you found a job yet?" Sera asked as she took the paper off a muffin for Violet, even though the nine-year-old was doing the same right next to her.

"No, still looking," she lied as she set her plate of muffins on the counter.

"Have you tried at the Grog? I hear they're looking again, and it's close. And everyone loves the Grog," Maby jumped in, eyeing the stove. She didn't like sweets for breakfast.

"No, I haven't, but I'll try today." Agatha wondered when she would tell them she didn't need a job anymore. But she liked that they were concerned about her, helped her out. It wasn't as if she thought she could hide it forever; she just didn't want to say anything yet. Her place in the family was being the mess-up, and she wasn't ready to be responsible yet.

"I would stay away from the Grog. That place is disgusting. I could see if Jonas has anything at his office. Maybe Mom has something." Buzz gestured at their stepmom, who was head of HR at a law firm.

Agatha pointed out the obvious to the people who knew her best. "I am not a people person."

"You just don't try. And without food to throw on them, you might be okay." Harper might have meant it as a compliment, but it wasn't.

Agatha answered her by throwing a muffin at her, hitting her in the face. She decided she should have stayed in sports because she was good.

"Pick it up, Ag," Sera said in her mom voice.

"She asked for it." Agatha went around the island and picked up the muffin and tossed it in the garbage.

From this side of the room, she could see Chris standing in the doorway, just watching them. His brown eyes met hers across the room, and he nodded at her with a grin. When she nodded back, he backed away from the doorframe, all without anyone noticing … almost.

"No need to sneak out, sir. We all saw you!" Buzz yelled.

Christ took a step into the kitchen. "I didn't want to disrupt anything."

"Did you want something to eat?" Harper asked. "We have muffins, and if you wait long enough, there are stuffed pork chops, red potatoes, and dinner rolls."

"I want a dinner roll," Sera said with excitement. It wasn't an item always on the breakfast menu.

"I'll have a muffin, but then I'm off." He looked a little scared of the room full of women.

"Don't let us chase you off." Sera looked him up and down. "Okay, so I have to admit it right now, I like knowing which of you he belongs to. Years of guessing who was with who in the morning got old."

Agatha knew Sera had no idea who Chris was because she was sure her stepmom wouldn't have been so welcoming if she did. "He doesn't belong to me. He's trying to kill himself via his house, and I saved him from himself for a few hours. He didn't stay in my room."

"Why not?" Sera questioned, not acting motherly at all.

"How about we not talk about my love life, or lack thereof," Agatha answered, remembering what she didn't like about them all living with her—topics like this all the time.

Chris took a muffin and backed slowly from the room. "I'll leave. Thank you, Agatha."

When he was gone, all eyes turned to her, and suddenly she was the center of the conversation. With everyone looking at her, she wondered if the floor could swallow her, but since she wasn't at Chris's house, she knew it wouldn't.

Harper couldn't control her smile. "So, not into sports guys?"

"Agatha's having sex with Chris Lowell!" Maby said as if he was a movie star.

"Chris Lowell?" Sera questioned from beside Maby. Her voice said all the puzzle pieces were falling into place; she was the only one who knew about high school. "That is not how I ever pictured him," she added in a mumble.

"I am not having sex with him," Agatha said again. "He just spent the night, not in my room."

"Liar. I wouldn't *not* tap that," Buzz stated.

"Me either," Maby practically moaned.

"Anybody else?" Agatha asked her sisters and stuffed her hands in her pockets.

"Nope, I only have eyes for Harrison," Sera stated.

"I'm good." Harper pulled out the pan of pork chops from the oven.

"Okay," Agatha said and pulled her phone from her pocket. "So, which man am I calling first? Jonas or Cliff? Cliff or Jonas?"

Buzz dove at her, but since the woman was insanely pregnant, she was easily dodged. Maby was quicker, but Agatha got the dining room table between them as she dialed, choice made.

"Hey, Cliff!" She shifted quickly, keeping Maby across the table from her, but Maby was quick. "Christopher Lowell slept in Maby's bed last night."

Cliff laughed. "She slept with me, though."

"She admitted to wanting to have sex with him," Agatha said as Maby came over the table and grabbed her phone as she pushed her into the wall. Sitting on the floor in a daze, she had forgotten how agile the twins were when they needed to be. It reminded her of their childhood fights in the kitchen.

"Jonas wouldn't believe you anyway, Ag. I'm carrying his spawn, and I barely want to have sex with him right now. Call him," Buzz admitted defeat from her stool.

"I don't know if I can get up," Agatha admitted from the floor. Maby hit hard.

"Harper, go help Agatha up. Buzz and I can't anymore," Sera said before serving herself a pork chop.

Agatha scrambled to her feet before Harper made it over to her. Harper turned back to the food, saying, "At least she didn't give you a black eye this time."

"That was Lucy. But I really didn't want another one of those," Agatha agreed.

Sitting on the stool that Maby had abandoned, Agatha looked at the pork chops. She wanted one, but she'd already had a muffin. One breakfast was enough. Harper caught her looking, and without saying anything, grabbed a container from the cabinet, put two in, and tossed them into the fridge. Agatha wondered again if they were thinking she was getting fat.

"So, how did you end up with Chris Lowell in your house?" Sera asked not so innocently. She was prying.

"He tried to start his house on fire with bad wiring, blew the circuit breaker, and had no idea how to fix it. He came over for a flashlight."

"What time?" Harper asked with interest.

"Around two, when you texted me. What were you doing up at that time thinking about platters anyway?" Agatha tried to turn the conversation to her sister.

"Having sex with my man, then it hit me I needed those. I keep forgetting them here."

"Must be great sex if you were thinking about platters," Agatha teased.

Harper shrugged. "It was. We were in the pantry and knocked a few things down."

"Back to middle of the night," Sera said quickly, pointedly ignoring Harper's story. "What were you doing up at 2 a.m.?"

"Drawing, then getting sex platters." Agatha folded her arms. "His house is unlivable and might have asbestos everywhere. The dining room ceiling fell in. He's going somewhere else tonight."

"Too bad," Harper said.

"I don't like him," Sera stated flatly. "Stay away from him."

Both sisters looked at their mom. She had never said she didn't like a man. Over the years, she had obviously not liked some of the guys they brought home, but she had never said it, not once. Agatha knew why. It was the same reason she was staying away from him herself.

"I'm not his biggest fan either," Agatha admitted quietly.

Maby walked into the room and interrupted the silence. "I had to do a little sex talk on your phone, Ag, but I washed it off."

Agatha took the wet phone from her sister. Harper immediately took the phone and grabbed a container from the cabinet behind her. Dropping the phone in, she shook it to get the rice to cover it. This was not the first time a phone had been washed in the house over the years.

"I hate you," Agatha said.

"Don't tell Cliff I'm sleeping around. He gets jealous." Maby pushed her off the stool that had been hers earlier.

Agatha didn't fight back, letting her sister have her stool. It had been a little mean. Cliff was always jealous of men in Maby's life, though there weren't many, and she would never stray.

"What time do I have to be where tonight?" she asked Harper, referring to that night's catering gig.

Harper filled her in, then took her chicken and muffins and went home. Maby helped her to her car and also left. After an hour of chatting with Buzz and Sera about baby preparations, the night started to catch up with her. She should have forced herself to sleep after getting Chris settled.

After Buzz left, taking Violet for the day, Agatha had admitted she was tired. That left Sera alone with Agatha, not what she wanted after having Chris in her house.

"I don't want to be your mother, Agatha, but I am your mother. Stay away from Chris Lowell. It took you a long time to get over him last time. Too long. From what I hear, his life is not going well. You don't need that in yours."

"Don't worry; I have no intention of anything happening. We're just neighbors," she said.

"Keep it that way." Sera hugged her and left.

Watching her leave, Agatha was happy the lecture wasn't as bad as it could have been. Maybe Harrison had mellowed the woman.

The house was now empty, and Agatha went up the stairs to her bedroom. After a quick shower, she climbed into bed. Thoughts of Chris floated through her head as she let sleep overtake her. So maybe she was dreaming he was in bed with her. Was that a crime?

CHAPTER TWELVE

OVER THE WEEKEND, Chris found a hotel close by. Not that he had
wanted to; he wanted to stay with Agatha even if the kitchen would be
full of women when he woke up. He knew he shouldn't have stopped
to say goodbye, but he couldn't help himself. He had just needed to
see the woman one more time.

Everything that the women had said to him had been worth it to
see Agatha throw a muffin at the blonde. Then sarcastically call the
other blonde "mom." Agatha was great at sarcasm.

After he had left her house, he hadn't seen her again all weekend,
not even a glimpse. Not that he had been looking, he just happened to
notice that she wasn't outside. Not when he had spent three hours
trying to fix the railings on the porch. Not when he had decided to
remove the paint from the wainscoting in the front room, the one with
the big window facing her house. Not even when he had sat on his
porch as he ate not only lunch but also his supper. Not one glimpse
of her.

He would have thought that she wasn't even home, except there
were lights on in her house when it got dark. More lights than he
would have thought needed for a woman who lived alone. Or maybe

she had company, except there were no extra cars on the street. Not that he was looking.

Today, he should be cleaning the mess in the dining room or even in the bedroom upstairs. At first, he hadn't cleaned up because he knew how much work it was going to be, then it was due to the fear that just touching anything would kill him from unknown substances, something that he hadn't once thought of until Agatha said it. Now he couldn't stop thinking about the possibility.

Instead, he had spent his day going from one half-finished project to another, not doing anything substantial to any of them unless it was to make them worse. That had happened more than a few times.

So far, he hadn't finished a single project he had started in the house. When he had started each project, he had thought it was going to be easy. Then about an hour into it, he would realize he was in over his head. So, he would stop before he completely destroyed whatever it was. After more research, he realized he was missing a tool, or his project wasn't exactly like the one in the video, or he had just done something completely wrong. Sometimes all of the above.

He tried to not let it bother him. After all, wasn't there a learning curve on learning home improvement? So he made a few mistakes—it happened.

Stopping his progress on removing the kitchen floors, he headed for the front of his house. It was just after three in the afternoon. Stepping out onto his porch, he watched and waited.

As if on a timer, Agatha opened her door and slipped outside. What was it about this woman that made his heart skip a beat? Chris left his house wanting to talk to her. He wanted to see her up close again.

Once he had made his way across the street, she noticed him and smiled from her spot on the top of the steps. Her mail was at her side, and she was holding a can of pop, just like every day.

Her orange shirt said "Pin" in gold letters, the letters and the shirt clashing horribly.

"Hi, Agatha. Good news. No asbestos, so I'll live." He smiled. He had just gotten the call and thought she would be interested, which was why he had hurried over there.

Grinning back at him, she took a sip of pop. "Good, except the rest of the house is trying to kill you for hurting it so bad."

"I'm cleaning today and reassessing." If that meant procrastinating, then he wasn't lying.

"Hiring professionals?"

"If I didn't know you were joking, I would start taking your question to heart. Except I know that you believe I can complete my renovations on my own," he said. Ignoring the disbelief on her face, he continued, "Sorry about your friends thinking we slept together."

"Sisters," Agatha corrected and wondered if he remembered any of them from high school. "I don't think they think so anymore. I told them that you are destroying your house, and I am the only neighbor that lets you stay over when needed." She grinned, and he realized she was the only neighbor who had taken notice of him.

"They were your sisters? You don't look alike," he replied and realized he maybe shouldn't point that out. It wasn't like he and his siblings looked all that much alike. Okay, they totally did.

"I know. I'm the black sheep of the family, literally and figuratively." She grinned at her joke and then turned from him. "But I look like this one, don't I, Violet?"

"You do, we are sisters," Violet said and gave Agatha a hug.

"My favorite sister. How was your day today?" Her attention was turned to the little girl.

"Nick J. dumped glitter on me again. He keeps saying I'm sparkly." Violet didn't seem happy with the attention from the opposite sex.

"You are sparkly, baby girl. You get that from Mom." Agatha hugged the little girl to her again.

"Dad calls her bubbly." The girl didn't sound convinced but accepted the hug.

"Bubbly, sparkly, it's the same thing. Don't let Nick J. take that away from you, Violet. Don't let anyone take that from you," Agatha said as she looked over the girl's head. There was pain in her eyes.

She shook herself and got up to take the little girl into the house as usual. Neither invited him to go with, so he was left on the sidewalk.

He didn't understand the pain he saw on her face. After the door shut behind the pair, he went back to his house, but he couldn't get her sad brown eyes out of his mind. Someone had hurt her once, and he hated that person.

CHAPTER THIRTEEN

IT WAS close to midnight when Agatha made it home from waitressing with Harper. Lucy was still on maternity leave; despite that she had made most of the food that had been served. Tonight's crew had been her, Maby, and three strangers. Agatha couldn't believe Maby showed up to work since her husband was rich, but maybe she still did it for the same reason as Agatha: to spend time with her sisters.

Shutting off the car, she looked up at the house across the street and saw that lights were on. She wondered if he had destroyed anything else in the house since she had last seen it. Probably. It had been five days, and she had noticed him over there every day, so damage had most likely been done.

As long as his focus was on his house and not on her, she was fine. It had taken time, but she was now okay with him never remembering her. After all, once his house was renovated, he would be gone again. Him gone was all that mattered.

Slipping out into the dark warm night, she was glad she had shed the white long-sleeve blouse that Harper demanded the waiters wear. She had pulled on a neon green "File Done" shirt. Yes it was correctly spelled, but nobody knew who would want a shirt that said it. It was more comfortable than what she had been wearing all evening serving to rich snobs, even if Buzz and Jonas were in attendance. They were rich snobs, after all, since Jonas was a tech billionaire.

Agatha slammed her car door, happy to be home and done with work until Friday, when she had another gig with Harper. Until then, she was free, except from three to five every day when she was busy with Violet.

She headed toward her house until she heard a terrible, loud crash coming from the house Chris was destroying. Turning quickly, she hurried over there with phone in hand in case she had to call an ambulance. Pushing through the door, she couldn't see past the dust cloud that engulfed the entire entrance.

"Chris, are you okay in there?" she called, not wanting to venture inside until the dust settled.

"I'm okay," came from the stairway, or at least where she remembered the stairway being.

The dust started to settle, and Agatha took a deep breath and headed into the house to make sure Chris wasn't dying. The house did have it out for him, but with good reason. She looked around upstairs until she saw movement in one of the bedrooms, the one that was probably above the living room downstairs.

He was completely covered in white powder, from head to. The floor was covered in small and large pieces of plaster.

She couldn't stifle the laugh that erupted from her at the sight of perfect Chris Lowell covered in plaster and dust. He was busy shaking his body and using his hands to get the bigger pieces off him.

"Not funny, Agatha," he said from his spot in the middle of the room.

"Very funny, actually. The living room is destroyed." She leaned against the doorframe to watch.

He stomped his foot. "Shit. Again? That's what happened to the dining room."

"Did you do something to make the walls came down on you?" She laughed again at the image. He was probably big enough to make it happen.

"No, smartypants. I was taking down these wood pieces. They look weird." He kicked one that was on the ground.

"You mean the ceiling supports? I can see how those wouldn't seem important." She continued to laugh as she turned to leave. He was alive, so her job was done.

"You're going to just leave me?" he called after her.

"Yep. I don't want to be here when this thing just falls in on you." She headed for the stairs because she didn't need to tempt herself by being near him.

"Ag," he called again, stopping her in her tracks. Nobody called her that unless they were related to her. Not even the husbands were allowed to call her that, ever.

Spinning on her heels, she hissed, "Do not call me that. You are not allowed to call me nicknames."

He was following her and stopped at her words, his smile gone. "Sorry, Agatha. I won't call you that again."

"Just don't do it again." She turned to leave again.

"Agatha, wait."

Stopping, she turned back to him. "What?"

"I'm really sorry I called you that. I should have asked first." His words hit their mark, as if he knew it was him that made her hate when people called her anything but her given name. Him and his Chrissy, and her trying to be someone else, someone that in the end, she didn't want to be.

"It's okay, Chris. Maybe I'm a little oversensitive about it." She ran her hands over her face to keep him from seeing too much. "It's late, and I'm tired."

"Sorry I woke you," he apologized.

She shrugged. "You didn't. I was just getting home from work."

"Is there any way I could take a shower at your place? Mine are out of commission, and I can't really go get a hotel room like this." He almost leaned against the banister but shifted away from it quickly.

"Sure, you can stay in the same room if you want," she relented. He was right—he couldn't go into a hotel looking like he did. And if she locked herself in her room, she wouldn't even notice he was there.

Or she hoped she wouldn't notice. She turned away from him, walking down the stairs without touching any of the rails as she went.

Calling after her, he asked, "Will the house be full when I wake up?"

"No," she yelled back. "Just me tomorrow."

Out the door and across the street, she didn't stop until she was in her bedroom and had the door shut. Leaning against it, she forced herself to stop thinking. He was her past and should stay there. He had destroyed her at eighteen, and he didn't even know who she was today. Wasn't that enough reason for her to stay away from him?

Right now, she should be letting him die in the house that he was not so slowly killing. There was no reason that she should let him stay with her. He didn't deserve that. He didn't deserve to be near her at all.

But there was something about him that always made her feel protective of him. Though he was always bigger and stronger than her, she always felt there was something soft about him. It was part of his attraction.

Before she moved away from her bedroom door, she heard her guest shower turn on. Now she knew he was naked in her house again. Still, she wanted to join him, but she forced herself to shower in her own bathroom so that she could wash her awful thoughts away.

By the time she had washed him and her day off her body, the house was silent. Not wanting to stay up all night like she did the last time he stayed over, she forced herself into bed. Though she was not overly tired, she couldn't let herself leave her room that night. Even though he had hurt her time and time again, she would crawl into his bed and let him hurt her all over again. Because she craved him too much not to.

CHAPTER FOURTEEN

BRIGHT SUN WAS SHINING through the window when Chris woke up and rolled onto his back. Once again, he was back in Agatha's house because he was a moron. It had been almost two weeks since he started to flip his house, but so far, he had done nothing but destroy it. Agatha was probably right; he needed to hire professionals to fix it. He had no idea what he was doing.

Rolling out of bed, he was happy to find that the battle with the ceiling hadn't had any effect on his knee. Chris pulled on the clean pants he had brought and his blue Basten shirt. He really liked the shirt and wore it more than he liked to admit. Everyone asked him what it meant. Sometimes, he just made something up.

In the hallway, he looked into the open door of Agatha's room and saw that it was empty and the bed was made. He found her downstairs, sitting at the table with papers strewn around her. She was in blue jeans as usual and a gray t-shirt.

"Morning, Agatha," he said to the back of her head.

She turned at his greeting and said, "Morning. Did you sleep well?"

"Yes, Mabel has a nice bed." He pointed to the coffee pot, she nodded, and he filled himself a cup.

"Maby always got all the nice stuff around here," Agatha complained with a smile as he sat down in the chair near her.

"Maybe?"

"Mabel's nickname is Maby. Only to the family, though. Everyone else calls her Mabel or Mabel Lucie. She goes by both." She gathered up her papers and put them into a pile. Her shirt said, "Grand Cannon."

"Lucy, the one who can't spell?" Taking a sip of the bitter drink, he remembered her telling him Lucy was the one who made all the shirts. He remembered everything Agatha had ever told him.

"You remember her name?" Her brown eyes were looking at him, then she shook her head. "No, Mabel Lucie and Lucy Maud are twins."

"That's not confusing at all." He chuckled a little at the overly twin names.

"They're identical, so gets even more confusing."

"Do you have a twin?" he asked.

"No, just me." Agatha pushed the papers away from him.

"It's just you, but there's seating for over a dozen in here." He looked around the room. She was back to acting prickly. Looking back, he couldn't pinpoint what he had said to change her mood.

"I have six sisters, and four are married. Then there's Mom and Harrison. Lucy has twin babies now, and Buzz and Mom are both pregnant." She listed off enough people to fill the room beyond capacity.

"Your mom is pregnant?" He looked at her closely, wondering how old she was. Maybe she was younger than he had thought. He couldn't imagine his parents having any more kids, even before his dad had died.

Chuckling, she got up, taking the papers with her. "Stepmom. She was young when she married my dad."

"You call your dad Harrison?" he questioned.

"No, Harrison is Sera's second husband. My dad took off with another woman when I was in junior high. Sera raised us." She leaned against the counter across the room from him.

"My parents split my senior year of high school. It was rough," he admitted, turning his chair to look at her, he liked to learn about her.

Rough wasn't even half of how bad it had been. Mostly because his mom had shielded him and his siblings from the worst of their father's bad qualities. From sleeping around to ignoring his family until the divorce, Chris hadn't seen it. Then his mom stopped covering for him, and it was suddenly all there for Chris to see. And then he couldn't unsee it.

"It usually is." She didn't elaborate.

"The little girl is Sera's then?" he asked, wanting her to say more.

"Yes." Her eyes lit up as she smiled. "Violet is Sera all over again, but she looks just like Harrison."

"I thought she was your daughter when I first saw you," he admitted.

Agatha toyed with her coffee cup. "No, I'm not mother material, never have been. I'm just good with some kids."

"You're more than good with her. She loves coming over here. I can tell." Every time he saw them together, it was clear Agatha was devoted to the little girl.

"She has to. Emma doesn't want to watch her, and I have nothing else going on. I've been watching her since she was a baby. She's about to get tired of me." Running her hand through her hair, she got up to fill her coffee cup again.

"She seems to like you a lot still." He got up from his chair and pushed it in.

He wanted to go over to her and hug her to take her pain away, but he knew she would never let him do it. All he wanted to do was make her realize that she was perfect, and her sisters knew that. That Emma was just going through a stage and would one day realize she needed her sister again.

"She's nine. By the time she's twelve, she'll think I'm lame." She picked up her coffee and took a drink, her eyes on the cup and not him.

"You are not lame, Agatha. Even your clothes are interesting." He pointed at her shirt.

"Lucy made it, not me." She shrugged and set down her coffee cup. "You can let yourself out."

Before he knew what was happening, Agatha had left the room, leaving him alone in her kitchen. While taking his coffee cup to the dishwasher, he dumped hers and put it inside also. Once again, he looked around the kitchen. It was so quiet that morning, so different than the last time he had been there.

Chris didn't see Agatha when he left the house. She must have gone upstairs or maybe even outside. Whichever it was, she wasn't anywhere around for him to thank her for letting him stay with her again. Maybe he would be able to see her when she waited for Violet today. He couldn't wait.

CHAPTER FIFTEEN

THE OPENING STRAINS of "Girls Just Want to Have Fun" rang through the house, announcing it was 2:55 p.m. The song meant it was Wednesday, but Agatha hadn't found a good Wednesday song yet, so this one would have to do. Setting down her mulberry purple pencil, she headed downstairs to meet Violet, singing as she went.

Agatha loved this song and remembered when her family would belt out the lyrics every time it came on the radio. Nobody tried to restrain themselves as they sang along together.

Feeling content, Agatha set out the cookies she had taken from the freezer that morning before Chris had woken up, she was happy Lucy was still providing baked goods even with the babies in the house. Agatha didn't bake. Ever. But then again, two of her sisters were chefs, so she didn't have to.

Grabbing her pop from the fridge as the second chorus rolled around, she sang and headed for the door to wait for Violet. Movement in front of her made her scream and drop her unopened can on the floor.

Chris was leaning against the open front doorframe, watching her. Yelling to make the music stop, she stood staring at him as he chuckled.

"Keep singing, Agatha. I always wondered how you managed to walk outside at the same time every day. You have a timer."

"Shut up, Chris." Agatha blushed with embarrassment. She had enjoyed singing to the radio as loud as she liked now that she lived alone. Except now she would forever think that Chris was watching her and acted like it was a joke. "What are you doing here?"

"The mailman dropped off a box at my place by mistake, so I brought it over." He held up the box. "Miss Lovely."

Stiffening, Agatha wondered if he would make the connection now that he knew her last name, that everything would suddenly fall into place for him. He seemed to remember everyone's name but hers. That alone should show her that he was not worth her time.

"Thank you." She stomped up to him and took the box from his hands. She knew what it was and didn't want Violet to see it. Not yet.

Opening the closet by the front door, she tucked the box in there. The little girl wouldn't look in there. Agatha would look at it after Violet had gone home.

"Is it a secret?" He nodded at the door.

"No, just not something Violet has to see."

"Adult stuff?" He winked.

"My stuff," she stated before going outside to wait for Violet on the step, pushing past Chris's warm hard body as she went.

"Touché." He followed her out of the house.

"It's just my business, okay? I don't go snooping around your falling-down house, do I?" She sat down, not bothering to get the mail today and leaving her pop still on the floor in the living room, unopened.

"Sorry I said anything. You're in a bad mood today," he said but didn't leave.

"Really? You came into my house, Chris. You laughed at me," she said the words more to herself as she hugged her knees to her chest. He didn't care about laughing at people. Nobody ever laughed at him.

He sat down next to her on the front step and put his arm around her. "I just thought that you were cute, Agatha. So cute and sparkly that Violet was coming over. I'm sorry I laughed at you. I should have just sung along because girls do just want to have fun."

Sighing, she let him hold her against his big body. She could have sworn that he kissed her hair, but she wasn't going to go there. It was bad enough that she liked being in his arms again, being close to him, smelling him. The longer they sat, the more her body wanted from him, even if it was just a touch.

Looking down the street, she saw Violet skipping their way. She was chatting to herself or her imaginary friend. Today in Chris's arms, she saw him, their baby. His blond curls were in contrast to Violet's dark hair. Pushing out of his arms, she rushed into the house away from Chris and the images of their son, a son he never knew about or wouldn't even care about.

Even though she didn't even get to see him, he was so much a part of her life. She thought about him often, and that he and Violet would have been the same age didn't help.

She tried to pull herself together; Violet needed her strong. For two hours, she needed to be strong for Violet. Then she had all night to fall apart. After washing her face in the bathroom, she came out to see Chris and Violet at the kitchen island.

"There she is. I told you she was here." Chris pointed at her with half a cookie.

"I'm here. Sorry, Violet," Agatha apologized.

Violet shrugged. "It's okay. I was telling him that sometimes you aren't on the step but in the house somewhere."

Running a hand over her hair, Agatha was mad at herself for letting her emotions get the best of her. This was her Violet time, and nothing got in the way of that. Not even Christopher Lowell.

"Not often," Agatha stated. She took her job seriously.

"Sometimes you're sleeping. Then I get to wake you up, like Buzzy does." The kid grinned wide.

"How does Buzzy wake her?" Chris asked the little girl.

"With a bucket of water. *Cold* water." She giggled.

"Sounds mean," Chris said.

"I started it, so I guess it's my fault," Agatha admitted. Sometimes having four sisters wasn't easy.

"Didn't think that one through?" Chris popped the last of his cookie in his mouth.

"I didn't think everyone would still be living here as they approached their thirties." She shrugged. They actually had more fun together after they were all out of their teens than during them. There had been way less taking things seriously once they turned twenty.

Chris turned from them and went to the fridge, then grabbed out a pop and set it down in front of Agatha. Agatha looked at it as if it might bite. The action was so unexpected of him, and she didn't want to think of him as that thoughtful. Instead of dwelling on it, she sat on the stool nearby and opened it.

Chris looked around. "Must have been crazy in here with five grown women."

"Six, counting Mom and Emma and Violet here. It was a madhouse sometimes, but it's quiet now." She looked around the room, too, recalling the fights and make-ups that followed.

"What is your favorite memory of living here, Violet?" he asked the little girl.

She scrunched up her brow and thought. "When Mom started the food fight, and everyone joined in and there were potatoes everywhere."

"That took hours to clean, and I still find odd foods around the house." She loved her sisters, and they loved food until it all turned to hate, and it started to fly.

"Food fight." Chris grinned at her.

"Yup, though Maby tackling Ag last weekend was fun."

Agatha pulled her phone from her pocket. Maby had shut it off before its bath, which sometimes helped. This was one of those times.

"I would have liked to see that." Chris was looking right at her as if he could see it happening.

"You just missed it. Ag called Cliff and told him you were sleeping in Maby's bed. Then Maby dove over the table and tackled Ag to get her phone away from her." Violet laughed.

"She can hit hard when she wants to." Agatha shrugged and accepted that he knew it happened now.

"Are you excited to be a big sister, Violet? Since you're so used to being a little sister?" Chris turned his attention to Violet, ignoring the funny story. Was it because she had overreacted when he had laughed at her?

"Yes, even though it is a boy. He won't be the first boy in the family, but I don't know when there will be another girl," Violet told him, all serious.

"Boys can be fun too," Chris said.

"No, they cannot. Boys are annoying." Violet crossed her arms.

"I bet baby brothers are probably fun."

"Do you have a brother?" Violet asked him.

"Yes, a younger brother and older sister." He told her.

"Is your brother annoying?" Violet asked, taking a third cookie from the plate, though she knew the two-cookie rule.

"Yes, he is. I guess you're right." Chris threw up his hands. "Agatha, is there any way I could do a load of laundry before I have to walk around naked? I know that is against the rules."

"You wouldn't be the first to break that one," Agatha admitted.

"You?" Chris asked.

She blushed at his scrutiny. "Very rarely."

"So yes?" he asked, looking at her shirt.

"I was young and crazy once." She got up to get away from his prying eyes.

"Was she crazy once, Violet?" he asked.

"Nope, I don't remember her ever being crazy," Violet lied for her, like a true sister.

"Yes, you can do a load of laundry, but do not break my machines. Or anything else. Did you want me to just do it?" she said, starting to worry that he would destroy her house since it seemed he was almost completely done with his own.

"Haha, Agatha. I'm perfectly okay doing my own laundry." He walked away from them, but Agatha knew he would be back soon. So much for spending a few hours with Violet and then letting her emotions take over. Now she would have to wait until his laundry was done before that could happen.

CHAPTER SIXTEEN

IT HAD BEEN years since Chris had watched cartoons with a kid, not since he was a child himself. And never had he watched them with anyone as sarcastic as Violet. She back-talked the entire show. Then she'd criticize the colors and the graphics, pointing out flaws for two entire shows.

Agatha, for her part, sat on the other couch and encouraged the kid. She saw these flaws also. It was like they watched the shows to catch the flaws, not to watch cartoons. He wondered if that was how he was when he watched a football game. It was super annoying.

One load of laundry was done and folded on the chair in the corner. The other load had about a half an hour left. Then he could leave the sisters to nitpick the shows on their own.

After a few minutes into the new cartoon, the front door opened, and a tall dark-haired guy in a suit walked into the house without knocking. Chris wondered who he was for only a moment until he realized that the little girl looked just like him.

"Daddy!" she yelled and jumped off the couch, running to him. She hugged him tight. "Agatha, Chris, and I were watching cartoons. Chris didn't realize that there were mistakes."

"Christopher Lowell." Chris got up to shake the man's hand. "I guess I always just watched them for entertainment, not to analyze them," Chris admitted. It seemed the man didn't even blink at having a strange man spending time with his stepdaughter and daughter in the middle of the afternoon.

"Harrison Dean. I still don't see it," Harrison Dean said with a smile. "But Violet is an artist, and she notices it."

"I do, Harrison. Is Mommy home?" Violet grabbed her backpack from where she had thrown it when she came in earlier.

"Yes, she is. Just too tired to come and get you. So I get to," Harrison told his daughter, then turned to Agatha. "Thanks, Agatha. See you tomorrow probably."

"See you tomorrow, Harrison." Agatha stayed on the couch.

When the door had shut, Chris turned to her as she shut the TV off. "Is he her dad? She called him Harrison."

"He is her dad, but he's only known about her for about a year. Long story," Agatha said, leaning back in the couch cushions.

Chris sat back down on the couch next to Agatha. Her eyes didn't open. "Tired?"

"Yes, I had to save a man from his house again in the middle of the night." Her eyes remained closed. "Is your laundry done?"

"Close, but not yet," he replied, watching her. He reached over the back of couch, needing to touch her hair again, to feel the silky strands on his fingers. There was something about her that captivated him, that drew him in.

Since the first day he had met her, he had the odd sensation that he had known her his entire life but had no idea who she was. When he had hugged her on the steps earlier, his body had immediately said, "Her, I want *her*. This is her." Never had he had that feeling before.

Touching the black hair, he realized she was probably asleep when she didn't move away from his hand. Tucking her hair behind her ears, he noticed that she used to have more earrings in her ears than the four she currently wore. Way more.

Her last name was Lovely, the same name as the Chris Lovely from high school. He'd have asked if she was related to her or not. Or even if he knew her. But part of him didn't want to ask because then he would have to admit how awful he had been to the other woman. He didn't want Agatha to see who he had been. A part of him never wanted to run into Chris again, because whenever he did, it always ended with him acting like an ass. He was tired of being an ass around that woman.

He was starting to feel like an idiot, so he stopped touching her and went to get his laundry from her basement. Earlier, Violet had showed him the way to the laundry room and had showed him the totes of shirts in the basement. She also informed him that she didn't think anyone had sex in the basement, but that every other room someone had probably had sex in it. He knew from her words that she had no idea what the adults were saying or doing but heard everything they said.

Up the stairs with his clothes, he saw Agatha was gone from the couch, and he didn't find her on the main floor either. Deciding not to look for her further, he left his clean clothes, hoping to sleep in Maby's bed again, and headed to his place to see what work he could do.

Once inside his house, he knew there was nothing for him to fix. He had destroyed as much as he could. All that was left was trying to figure out how to get it back to what it was. Making it better wasn't even an option anymore without actual help. A lot of actual help.

CHAPTER SEVENTEEN

A NAP always did wonders for Agatha's mood. In fact, the nap, which lasted three hours, was exactly what she needed after seeing Chris today. Suddenly she couldn't go anywhere without him being there, and that included her house. He was like a stray cat she had fed, and now she couldn't get rid of him.

Before heading downstairs to find something to eat, she tossed on gray sweatpants and a purple T-shirt. In the kitchen, she was happy with a few leftovers from the Tuesday night benefit she had worked. Just some chicken in a sauce with potatoes, but she wasn't picky.

Waiting for the microwave to do its magic, she went to the entryway and grabbed the box she had put there hours before when Chris had caught her singing. She opened the box and laid out the three books from inside on the counter. They looked perfect, just how she had envisioned them as she drew them. *Porcupine's Adventure*, *Turtle's Walk*, and *Lost Kangaroo* by Christie Lovely.

Looking at the author name, she still regretted not using her own a little. But Agatha sounded so old, and Christie felt kid-friendly. Now she wished she hadn't done it. A.C. Lovely would have been better, but it was too late now.

She took the books to the third floor and placed them on a shelf in the back corner. Now there were nine. Eight months after the first was published, she had nine books out in the world. If she hadn't missed that meeting the night she had slept with Chris, she would have had these published a year before. Instead, she had waited another seven months to go to that meeting.

Happy with her little library, she went back down the two flights of stairs to the kitchen to eat her supper in peace and quiet. She grabbed a pop and pulled the chicken from the microwave and set it all on the counter. Taking her first bite, she saw the mortgage paperwork on the counter across from her. Getting up again, she grabbed the papers and looked over them again. Nothing unusual that she could see, except that the current owner wanted to meet her on Monday morning before the papers would be signed. Her dad was the owner, as far as she knew, and he hadn't wanted to see her in years. Why now? It didn't matter because she would meet with anyone to get her house.

Running her fingers over the words, she wondered if her father was actually going to be there. She hadn't seen him since she was in the sixth grade. She couldn't even remember what he looked like anymore. Was he light and fair like Harper or darker like the twins? What she knew was that he didn't look like her or Buzz, nor did their mom. The red hair could be explained away as a genetic fluke, but her own black hair was harder to justify. Even before he had left the family, she knew he probably wasn't her father.

Looking back, she didn't feel like he her treated her differently than her sisters. He had treated them all like kids he was stuck with working a lot and reading in his room when he was home. The girls were basically raising themselves when Sera had shown up. At nineteen, she didn't know how to treat the wild kids, so she just went with it. She let them do what they wanted unless it interfered with school or, later, work.

Never did Sera push the girls to go to college like she was pushed by her own parents. She saw them each for who each were. Harper went to France to study cooking, and Lucy worked in restaurants, doing the same thing, knowing each had their own path. Maby was school-bound forever, but her twin Lucy was not. Buzz had gone to school, then had a hard time finding a job that was a good fit for her. But Agatha always felt she was the hardest one for Sera to understand —art wasn't Sera's thing. But Sera had never pushed Agatha to get a real job or even keep various bartending gigs.

Monday would come soon enough, yet Agatha had no idea what she was going to talk to her father about. Probably nothing. He called Sera once a year to check on them. If he wanted to talk to her, he could call the house.

Halfway through her meal, there was a knock on the door. Checking the clock, she saw it was almost 9 p.m., not a time for company, and her sisters did not knock. Agatha had an idea who it was.

Opening the door, she said, "What do you want, Chris?"

He grinned at her. "I was hoping Maby would let me use her bed again. Should I ask Cliff first?"

That made her smile. Cliff's jealousy was completely unfounded, but Agatha loved that the man would fight for her sister.

"Go ahead. Any floors in that house of yours anymore?" She looked across the street as he came into her house, filling it with his presence and his scent. Her nap had not been long enough to cleanse him from her mind.

"Thanks, Agatha. I will have you know that I am hiring a contractor tomorrow." He said with a smile, even if he was admitting defeat.

"What prompted that?" She bit her lip to stop smiling herself.

"This amazing woman across the street keeps telling me to. I decided to listen to her."

"She sounds smart."

"She would tell me she is. Thanks again, Agatha. I don't know what I would do without you," he said and headed right up to the room with all his stuff in his arms.

Shrugging, she decided this was maybe going to be easy if he was just going to bed when he came over. No need to worry about inter-acting with him or analyzing his every action. Instead, she wouldn't even see him in the evening, which was fine with her. Heading back into the kitchen, she debated on heating the chicken again but decided she didn't want to waste the time and ate it cold.

Agatha stacked the papers from the lawyer up, making sure the top page was blank. She had gotten used to nobody being around most of the time. If she wanted, she could have spread her stuff around the house, but she hadn't. The house looked just like it had for years, just with fewer people in it.

"Shoot, I was going to order us something in, but you already ate." Chris came into the kitchen in clean, sexy jeans and a tight gray T-shirt.

"Sorry. I had leftovers." She pointed at the plate in front of her.

"Do you have more?"

"Not of this, but you can look in the fridge and see if there's anything you want. Harper left pork chops on Saturday." She pushed the plate away from her. Chicken was not interesting anymore now that he was filling the room.

"And Harper is?" He pulled out a plastic container and put it on the counter.

"My sister, the blonde you talked to on Saturday morning. Not the pregnant one, that was Mom. Harper's a chef." She got up and took the container from him, placing it in the microwave.

"A chef? So this is chef-quality leftovers?" He looked into the microwave over her head.

"All my leftovers are. Lucy's a chef as well. Well, she's more a baker, but she can make anything Harper can." She shrugged, looking at his chest as he watched the food in the microwave.

"I might have to take all my meals over here." He looked down at her.

"Just don't destroy my house." Breathing was getting hard with him so close.

"I promise not to touch anything in your house, Agatha." He slid her hair behind her ears with his fingers, caressing the backs of her ears and making Agatha's breath catch. Her eyes snapped up to his.

"Good." It was all she could force out of her mouth. He was so close, and now he was touching her.

Knowing he was going to kiss her, it should have been automatic for Agatha to stop him. But watching his lips lower to hers, she found she wanted the contact so bad she pushed up on her tiptoes to meet him. His hands were cupping her face as their lips met gently at first. Delicate, soft, and warm.

His hands tilted her face, and she felt his wet tongue run along the seam of her mouth. She wanted to let him in even if she knew it had turned out badly in the past, but she wanted so badly to taste him again. It had been so long.

Her hands had slid up his chest when the microwave buzzer went off. He paused and looked up at it, dismissing the food and went back to kissing her. Agatha pulled him as close to her as she could. She needed him to surround her.

Pulling his mouth from hers, he trailed kisses to her ear, making her shiver at the memory of him doing it before and knowing what was going to happen—wanting what was going to happen.

Running his hands down her body, he cupped her butt and lifted her onto the countertop. Once she was settled, he slipped his hands under the hem of her T-shirt as his lips landed on hers again.

Wrapping her legs around him to pull him closer, she grabbed the material of his shirt and clung to him. His tongue probed her lips for a heartbeat before she let him in. Moaning, she remembered and memorized his taste at the same time.

Her fisted hands dragged the shirt from his body but didn't want to stop kissing him long enough to take it off. Instead, she bunched the fabric up and ran her fingers over the muscles that she craved, needing to touch him. Her hips ground against his, pressing her need into his obvious desire.

With his hands caressing her breasts, she moaned and arched her back, wishing he'd never stop. His lips trailed a path across her cheek and down her neck, then his hands were gone as he pulled her shirt over her head. Agatha fully approved and followed suit, pulling his shirt off and tossing it on the floor.

Pressing her bare chest to his, she sought his lips again. Her tongue probed the corners of his mouth, and her hands found his hair.

One of his hands was splayed across her back, and the other had slipped into her sweatpants and was kneading her bare ass. No longer was she sitting on the counter. Her entire being was wrapped around him, unable to get close enough.

Dragging her lips from his, she sucked in a breath, filling her lungs with him. Somewhere deep in her mind, something was telling her to get away from him, that this wouldn't end well. It never did with Chris.

"Agatha." His lips instantly he found that sensitive spot on her neck that cleared her mind of anything but him.

"Chris, I need you." She didn't recognize the voice or the words but knew they were all from her.

Maybe she would regret it all later. But for now, she was exactly where she had spent her lifetime dreaming about: being the person Chris Lowell wanted. Even for just a moment. Again.

CHAPTER EIGHTEEN

CARRYING AGATHA FROM THE KITCHEN, Chris stopped every few steps to kiss her, touch her, or shift her so that she knew how much he wanted her. He almost didn't make it up the stairs when her nails dug into his back when he shifted her enough to slip her pebbled nipple into his mouth. Her back arched and threw him off balance enough that he had to press her against the wall to steady them.

With her back against the wall, he slid his hands into her loose-fitting sweatpants until her legs dropped from around his waist so he could slide them off her. Dragging her panties off at the same time left her completely exposed to him.

Not wasting the opportunity, he ran a finger over her slick heat, making her moan. Chris loved how responsive she was. He teased her with his fingers as he bit down lightly on her nipple. Grabbing his head, she held him to her breast as her hips ground down on his fingers.

"Please, Chris," she panted between moans.

With a flick of his thumb over her clit, he felt and heard her suck in a breath as tremors overtook her body. All he could do was continue what he had been doing, making her completely lose control in his arms as tremors turned into spasms each time his thumb circled over her hard bud. He kept going until she jerked under his touch, and her hold on him relaxed as she came with his name on her lips.

Before he could rip his own pants off and sink into her right there on the stairs, Chris grabbed her limp body tight to him and walked up the remaining steps to the second floor. Getting inside her was all he could think about, to make her come while he was inside her.

The room he'd been sleeping in was well over ten feet down the hallway, but Agatha's was right there. So nice and close, and after how many times he had fantasized about being in there, he wanted to make it a reality.

He didn't take the time to look around Agatha's room, just set her in the middle of the brown bedspread, dislodging a pile of folded laundry in the process, sending the stack to floor. Her arms were around him, and she held him for half a moment longer than necessary before they flopped down above her head.

Unrestrained, he started kissing down her body again, this time with the ability to look and touch every inch of creamy bare skin he wanted to—which was all of it.

His cock was throbbing under his jeans, demanding attention. As if Agatha herself could hear it, she sat up, and her hands reached for the button on his jeans. Her hands slipped over his stomach, but he arched away.

His need to have her fingers on his cock was strong, but he realized he wasn't ready for them to be done yet. For the first time in his life, he felt that what they were doing wasn't sex; it was something more. Something to savor, something not to be rushed.

Grabbing her arms, he pulled them above her head and leaned down to kiss her. Those kissable lips had been on his mind since the first day he had seen her. Now they were his to explore, to taste.

Letting go of her hands, he touched her nose with his and whispered, "Leave them."

Her only response was a whimper, but they stayed above her head, buried below the dozen pillows leaning against her headboard.

"I want to savor you, starting at this scar that I want to know all about." He kissed the faint mark that was almost always hidden by her dark bangs. Then his hand ran down her leg until it grabbed a pair of socks that had managed to stay on the bed when all the other clothes were gone. "To these crazy sexy fuzzy socks."

Single-handedly, he pulled the socks apart and tossed one on the floor. He ran the other sock up her leg, the softness lightly grazing her body. He trailed it from her thigh, skimming the dark hair that covered her sex. Her whimpering started in earnest as he slipped past to her flat stomach. Circling her belly button, he watched her bite down on her lower lip, hard.

Kissing her until she released the lip from her teeth, he slipped the sock back over her core and swallowed the whimper that escaped her. Pulling away when her lips were safe from damage, he watched her nearly black eyes as the sock slid over her hard nipples over and over again, not breaking eye contact as her fisted hands crushed a small pillow to the top of her head, the only outward sign that he was having any effect on her.

Running the sock over her chest and neck, she crushed the pillow under her fingers. Then he slipped it over her face, brushing her lips, then kissing the lips, then again with the sock, kiss, sock. Until she whimpered again.

Every whimper caused his cock to strain more and more painfully against his jeans. As much as he was torturing her, he was doing worse to himself. Not that he cared; he loved every one of those whimpers.

Running the sock over her forehead, he asked, "How did you get this scar?"

Her voice was husky as she watched the sock brush her skin. "Harper, toaster, fourteen."

Another sweep. "Your sister threw a toaster at you when you were fourteen?"

Her only answer was another whimper as the sock disappeared from the scar and reappeared again on her breasts, only to run over her nipple, down her stomach, and over her core again. He ran it down her left thigh, all without breaking eye contact. "What about this one?"

Her only answer was to shake her head, the pillow moving with it since it was pressed so tightly to it.

"You don't know, or you are not telling?"

He dropped the sock and ran his bare finger over the inch-long white mark. The touch was so soft and delicate, as if he was concerned with hurting her. A whimper went through her again.

Her voice was shaky as her leg moved, trying to get his finger to touch her where she wanted him. "A guy I was with thought I was into pain."

Shimmying down the bed, he slipped between her legs, and all his attention went back to the scar. He hated that it represented a man who hurt her, that there was something marring her body that someone had intentionally put there.

Suddenly, it dawned on him that he had once been just like the guy, doing what he wanted to do and not carrying about the woman he was doing it with. The mark on Agatha was a reminder of who he had been and who he never wanted to be again. A part of him he never wanted Agatha to even see.

"Never again, Agatha. Never again will I let anyone do that to you. I won't let anyone hurt you." He looked into her eyes and promised.

Leaning down, he kissed the mark, then licked it before kissing it again, making it his own and taking away any thought of anyone else with her. He hated that anyone had been with her before him

Running his tongue over the mark, he let it slip further up as her whimpers grew louder until she was begging with his name on her lips. Unable to deny her any longer, he ran his fingers through her wetness a moment before his tongue, teeth, and mouth followed.

Begging and pleading instantly turned to moans and tremors, the same as she had on the stairs. Except this time, he could watch her face. As she got closer, her head started to toss back and forth, and her fingers gripped the pillow.

After only just one time with this woman, he knew when she was close. Her entire body started to shake, and her knees clamped around his head.

Sucking her into his mouth, he slipped a finger into her core. Her body jerked as she let out a scream, and the pillow above her head exploded into a cloud of white fluff.

As her body pulsed, he watched her head shaking back and forth as her hands clenched at the bedspread. With speed he didn't know he still possessed, he wrenched his pants and underwear off. With only enough sense to grab his wallet from the jeans before they hit the floor, he pulled out a condom.

After rolling it on, he watched her open her eyes and then slid into her. With her eyes suddenly open and on him, he leaned down and kissed her deeply. He kissed her until he couldn't be still any longer.

Then he started to slowly pump into her. Each thrust was met by a throaty sigh until they turned into gasps when he couldn't go slow anymore. He needed to feel her come around him. With his hands on her hips, he thrust into her faster and harder.

Her legs wrapped around him, and he could feel her tremor, knowing she was getting close. With all his concentration on her coming, he forgot his own needs for a moment until her body started to quake and grip his cock, causing him to come instantly.

Sated, he rolled to the side so that he wouldn't crush her. Then he rolled until he was on his back, and he wrapped his arms around her damp body, loving how perfectly she fit with his.

She rested her head on his chest, and with one hand on her back and the other on her ass, he made sure she stayed. Not that either was moving after that. They laid there for a long time before she gave a little shiver and sat up.

Agatha looked around the bed in question before touching his face. Her fingers came away with a little bit of the fluff.

"What is this?"

Chris smiled at her. She didn't even realize the pillow had been sacrificed during their love-making. He hoped it wasn't special.

"You ripped apart a pillow." He wiped some of the fluff off her chest. Her nipples instantly hardened at his attention.

"I wouldn't do that," she argued.

"Then it snowed in here."

"Don't be silly. What happened?"

"I wish there was a recording so that I could show you. A replay."

"Replay." Shaking her head, she sat up and brushed some fluff from her arms.

He rolled her over and pinned her to the bed. "I guess I'll have to do it again."

"You can't," she said with a smirk.

"I will." He promised and brought her hands over her head.

Agatha sighed. "Good luck. I'm spent."

Looking around, he found the sock and held it up. "We can start with the sock."

She whimpered, and he knew he definitely could make her come again. Apparently, his cock was on the same page.

"You remember this sock, right?" he asked and ran the sock again over her core, which caused her hips to jerk and for her to say his name as if he had been doing it for hours already.

"Say you remember, Agatha." He held the sock inches above her body. Her hands plucked another pillow from the pile and it was already firmly pressed to her head, this one smaller and harder to misshape.

"I remember," she said so breathlessly he barely heard it.

"Say you remember the sock making you break your pillow," he said, running the sock over her core again. "Or do I have to make you come again?"

With a jerk of her hips, she hissed, "Come again. Please, Chris, now."

At her sweet words, he couldn't tell her no. He couldn't even think of why he would want to. He positioned himself above her only to realize that he didn't have another condom.

"I don't have a condom." He sat back on his heels. He wasn't the kind of guy who would not wear a condom, no matter how drunk he was with a woman. So sober, he couldn't do it either. Even with Agatha.

Below him, Agatha threw the pillow against the wall and shimmied away from him. Pushing pillows as the went, she opened the night-stand drawer and pulled out a string of condoms.

She ripped open a packet and walked back to him on her knees. Pushing him back on his back, she rolled it on him and climbed on after. Slipping into her hot core was just as great as the last time, except this time she was in charge. All he had to do was lay there and let her do all the work.

Her body was instantly shaking, her hands on his chest as her nails bit into his skin. But still, he couldn't stop from coming when her body clamped around his.

Afterward, she lay on his chest as they tried to catch their breaths. She just lay there with her head on his chest.

Without picking up her head, she whispered, "I might have ruined a pillow."

Squeezing her butt cheek, he said, "I told you so."

Feeling her laugh was the last thing he felt until morning. Or until sometime in the night when he pulled the comforter around them. Even then, she didn't stir. He didn't even care that they were completely covered in pillow fluff. Morning would be soon enough to get that off in a nice hot shower. He just hoped she would join him.

CHAPTER NINETEEN

WALKING into her lawyer's office, Agatha realized she had only been here about three times. Most of their communications were over the phone or by letter. Though to be fair, she hadn't needed to renegotiate her contract with the publisher and had only needed her lawyer to draw up the paperwork for the purchase of the house.

Stopping at the reception desk, she said, "Christie Lovely to see Aspen Andrews."

"Take a seat," the woman replied, and Agatha took her chair. In this office, she was Christie again. It wasn't a persona she felt comfortable with anymore.

Becoming Chris's lover hadn't changed that; she was still a different person than she had been in high school. No matter who Chris was today, he was still the boy who showed her how cruel people can be. She could never become that naïve again.

"Nice to see you again, Christie," Aspen said, walking into the waiting room. "The seller is already here and waiting. I really didn't think they would want to meet you. It's very unusual."

"That's what I thought too," Agatha said. The knowledge that her dad was here and that she would see him for the first time in years was overwhelming.

"Okay, right in here." Aspen opened the door and Agatha's eyes went to the seller. But it wasn't her father sitting there, it was her mother. Not her real one, but Sera.

"Hello, Agatha Christie. I didn't really think I would see you this morning," Sera said, a red folder in front of her. The woman always color coded her files. Was red for anger or love? Agatha couldn't decide.

"I got the impression you two didn't know each other," Aspen said and took a chair with a manila folder on the table. "Mrs. Dean is the seller."

"Sit down, Agatha. Let's talk." Sera tapped the chair closest to her.

"Okay." Agatha couldn't think of anything more to say. This was not how today was supposed to go. Her dad was supposed to be a no-show, and then she would sign the papers. Now she had to talk to Sera.

"So, you want to buy my house. Why?" Sera said once Agatha's butt hit the chair.

"I didn't want to lose it when Dad died. I wanted to make sure that we never lost the house," she explained. Though she'd had the same thoughts since she was a teenager, she could now finally do it. In fact, it was the first thing she thought about buying when she started to make money. Everything else had taken a back seat.

"That's why I had your dad sign it over to me before Harper graduated." Sera pulled a tissue from her pocket and dabbed her eyes.

"Don't cry," Agatha said. "You can keep the house. I just didn't want Dad to have it anymore." She hugged her mom, who was a decade ahead of her in planning.

"Hormones." Sera returned the hug even more tightly than Agatha. "But I want you to have it. It's your and your sisters' house, not mine."

"Maybe we should talk to the girls about it," Agatha admitted. Now that it wasn't going to be sold to someone else, they had time for that.

Sera pushed her away. "No, they all have husbands who can buy them anything they want. I want you to have it."

"So, are we going forward with the sale?" Aspen opened her folder. "The purchase price was agreed on as $300,000. Is that correct?"

"Yes, I know it's lower than what it's worth, but I was hoping Dad wouldn't care." Agatha shrugged.

"He didn't. Do you have that kind of money, Agatha?" Sera looked at her.

"Yes."

"How? None of your jobs have paid more than starvation wages. And I don't think you've been working in months."

"I sold some of my art this year," Agatha finally admitted.

"Enough to hire a lawyer who isn't Harrison? And to buy a house? How much did you sell? All of it?" Sera demanded.

Agatha shrugged. "A few of the books I wrote for Violet. I found a publisher, and they liked them."

Yes, she should have told Sera when it happened, and right now, she wished she had, but it was never the right time. There had been a lot going on when she actually got the call; the family had other things happening. Or maybe she just let everyone else have happiness before herself. Because everyone would be happy for her and proud of her, but she hadn't allowed them to. Instead, she hadn't let them support her like she always did them.

"You've been hiding it from me for a year?" Sera was on the verge of tears, not that she wasn't always lately. But when her chin quivered, Agatha still felt awful about not telling her right away.

"It wasn't the entire year, just months, really. Besides, you were busy falling in love, getting married, then getting everyone else married or pregnant. That's a lot happening in a few short months. You haven't noticed much about me lately," Agatha said.

"I have too. You aren't the same person you used to be. You quit acting out, which I liked. You started eating and not looking dead, I liked that. You began being the kid you used to be when I met you, I liked that. I thought that if I said something, you would go back to being angsty Agatha. That's why I don't want you near Chris." Sera pushed Agatha's hair behind her ear as a tear fell down her cheek.

"I'm not going to fall for Chris again, Sera. I'm smarter than that now." Agatha hoped that would be true.

"Love doesn't care about how smart you are. Be careful," Sera whispered, wiping away another tear.

"I am. I don't let anyone into my heart, Sera. Ever," Agatha stated firmly.

Instantly, Agatha knew she had said the wrong thing when Sera drew in a sharp breath. Sera wanted her to find love, but not with Chris. Except Agatha was beginning to fear that her heart was only meant for Chris. It didn't matter how he treated it; it was his.

"I want you to, but not with him. Not again." Sera leaned in and hugged her tight, too tight.

"It's just fun. He will leave once his house is done, and then I'll get to say I'm completely over him." Agatha grinned and accepted the hug as she tried not to think about Chris leaving her again. But he didn't belong to her, and he never would. The past had shown her that, and they were not even a couple now. Whatever they were wasn't permanent.

Sera hugged her one more time and turned to Aspen. "I had my lawyer draw up paperwork for the sale. Everything is the same, except I changed the selling price to five dollars. The house was never mine; I was just holding it for the girls. Now one of them needs it, so it will be hers."

Aspen grabbed the paper and looked it over. She let Agatha sign, and by the time it was over, Agatha owned the big house she loved. Though her sisters would always be welcome and could move back in whenever they wanted to, Agatha would know they had a place to land when needed.

When everything was said and done, Sera took Agatha to the closest bookstore and bought her books, all six that were currently out. And nine copies of each one, one for each sister and one for herself. In true Sera fashion, they waited for nearly an hour as a worker scoured the back room to find enough copies. But Sera was determined to get a copy for everyone, including Louisa and Frankie in Chicago.

Since it was Sera, she told everyone in the bookstore who would listen that her daughter wrote and drew the pictures, nearly forcing everyone who got close enough to buy a book. Then she made sure that Agatha signed every copy available. The store workers just let it happen.

By the time Agatha made it home for the day, it was already almost time for Violet to come home. Sera had taken the day off after discovering that her daughter was an author. She invited everyone over to celebrate the books, even if Agatha didn't want to. There would be so many questions she didn't want to answer, so many jokes she didn't want to hear. Or was it because she had no idea how to be the sister with good things happening in her life? It had never been her before, and she didn't know what to expect.

Now she had to decide what she was going to do about Chris. If she invited him to go with her, he would know who she was and would not be happy. She was starting to think she should have told him a long time ago and was maybe digging a hole that might fall in on her.

Sitting on the step, she looked over at his house. There were two dozen men going in and out, trucks lining the block in both directions. It wasn't going to take long to fix his house with all these people.

She noticed his Turkish blue shirt first. She knew what it said, and she knew the hard muscles it hid. He saw her sitting there and flashed her a smile and a wave. Chris stopped what he was doing and walked toward her. All she could see was him; all she wanted to see was him.

As he walked across the street, she knew that she had not lied to her mom today. She didn't let anyone new into her heart. But Chris had never left; he had always had a small corner of it.

Her breath stopped at the knowledge that she was still in love with him, that she had never stopped. His smile made her just as weak-kneed as she had been at sixteen. His hands knew her body as well as they had when she was twenty-four. But for the first time in all those years, it seemed he liked her for her. Maybe it wouldn't last once he knew who she really was, but right now, he liked her.

"How was your day, Agatha?" he said from the sidewalk.

"Good, and yours?"

"Productive. Gary said he wanted to work late tonight to get the sheetrock up, so I am going to be late getting home." He grinned. Did he even notice that he had called her place home?

At least she didn't have to worry about inviting him to dinner. "That's okay. I'm heading over to Sera's for supper." No need to tell him the truth today.

"Shoot, I wanted to meet your sisters, but I need to be here for questions, and the flooring is being delivered. Tile for the kitchen."

"That will look nice."

"Are you heading over there after Violet comes?"

"No, Sera will meet her. I just had to drop some stuff off here, and then I'll go."

"Well, I won't keep you then. Have fun with your mom and sisters." He kissed her lips, right in the middle of the neighborhood where anyone could see.

"I will." She leaned her forehead into his and savored the moment. Not too many of these would be left after she told him.

"I am going to miss you." He ran his thumb over her lips.

"You won't even notice I'm gone." She bit her lip to not let it quiver at her words. She wondered if he felt it.

"I miss you every moment you're out of my sight, Agatha. I miss you now, and I still have you in my arms." His lips replaced this thumb for another kiss.

She stood up and pulled away from him. "I have to go."

Hurrying away from him, she didn't look back. His words were as empty has they had been when he was eighteen; she knew that. They were just something to make her feel special when she wasn't. He had perfected the game he had been playing for a decade, but she wasn't going to fall for it again.

Pushing into Sera's house, she was immediately engulfed by her sisters. Since only Maby had a day job anymore and even she had managed to cut back on her hours this semester, they were all there, hugging and laughing with her about her success and teasing her for hiding it from them.

It was what she needed: their high spirits to raise hers from the gutter. She didn't know why she couldn't just be happy to be in Chris's bed for a few weeks instead of dwelling on the future and the past and everything in between.

After she had signed all the books Sera had bought for the family, they all sat down and looked through them, oohing and aahing over the different drawings. It had been years since she had shown anyone in the family her drawings besides Violet. Maybe because they were in published books, they didn't have a bad word to say about them. Or maybe it was because they were all adults now and were more encouraging than when they were younger.

"So how long have you been published?" Maby, who was also a children's literature professor, was still flipping through the book on her lap.

"Since Thanksgiving week," Agatha admitted.

"And you still gave me socks for Christmas?" Buzz asked, grinning.

"Yes. They looked like your kind of socks." Agatha looked at her sister's fuzzy footed socks and tried not to remember Chris's erotic use of a very similar sock. She knew she was blushing but realized her sister probably thought it was because she was embarrassed about the books.

"You're right. But no socks next year. Maybe a car." Buzz fanned herself with a book, probably because she was wearing winter socks in September.

"Have Jonas buy you a car. I had to buy our house first." She said and knew Sera had already told them since nobody said anything about it, just nodded in agreement. With that off her chest, she decided to deflect the conversation. "And I have to save my money for my nieces and nephews. Anyone else planning to have one of those?" She looked at Maby and Harper.

Both shook their heads, but neither gave a verbal denial.

By the time the men showed up, Maby and Lucy were fighting about something, and Buzz was angry with Jonas for not buying her a car yet—same old sister squabbles. Agatha wished it were happening at her house; it always felt better when they were at her house.

Somehow, she had always assumed that when she told them, everything would change. That she would tell them she didn't need another job because she finally had a career, and suddenly, they would treat her differently. But telling them hadn't changed anything. She was still Agatha and still the same person she was before. Or maybe she had always been the same person in their eyes: jobless or published author, they loved her the same.

CHAPTER TWENTY

CHRIS TOOK a shower in Agatha's bathroom as he waited for her to come home from her mom's house. Though he knew where she was and how to get there, she hadn't invited him over. It was up to her to introduce him to her family. There was no way he was going to barge in again on her family time, especially after Violet had let slip that his being there once had caused Agatha to fight with her sister. He didn't want to be the reason she fought with anyone.

After the shower, he waited in her bedroom for her. Even after removing half a dozen pillows, he smiled at the pile still on the bed. There was still evidence of fluff on the comforter, and every once in a while, he'd see some land on the dresser or in the carpet. No matter how much cleaning up they had done that morning, there was just no way to contain the fluff. The problem with cleaning it up might have been his inability to keep his hands off her as they worked. They'd turned it into another round of seeing if he could get her to break another one. So far, no, but there was always tonight.

Now that he had touched her, he couldn't seem to stop. If she was close, he needed her closer. Not even just for sex, which had been what all his previous relationships had been about. With Agatha, he wanted to see the world through her eyes. Not just to hear her jokes and to make her laugh, but to know what made her sad so that he could make her world right again.

Being in her room was where he wanted to be when she returned home, so he figured he might as well just wait for her there. Not that he was opposed to having sex in other parts of the house, but he liked her here best.

Once all the pillows were on a pile on the floor, he sat down on her bed and pulled out his phone. With nothing to do, he searched for interesting football stuff. Nothing much happening despite the season starting. He had thought that even if he was busy with the house, he would still think about football and all that he had lost. Instead, all his concentration had been focused on trying to fix his house … and Agatha. She had taken up a good portion of his mind, even when he was working on the house.

Trying to not think about Agatha Lovely, he typed in the name he searched for every so often, but never found anything: Chris or Christie Lovely. The name never came up on social media. Never on any websites. Never even as a phone number. Nothing.

It felt wrong looking for information on another woman in Agatha's bed, but it wasn't like he was interested in Chris. Though they had sex more than once, he wasn't interested in her for that. He just wanted to apologize to her. It seemed he was destined to be a dick to one woman, and she was it.

He was so used to nothing coming up that when he typed in her name, he was surprised to get results. Books. Quite a few books written for children, but still books. Could they be by the same woman? The Chris he remembered had been an artsy girl. Looking deeper, he found no information about the author but decided he would buy her books one day and see if they gave any clues as to who the author was. Books usually had author bios in them, after all.

Hearing the front door open and close, he quickly turned off his phone and put it on the bedside table. All his focus was going to be on this Lovely, pushing the other one from his mind completely when he saw her walk into the bedroom. Her eyes landed on him and then looked away quickly, focusing on the other side of the room.

"Oh, I didn't think you would be here," she said from the doorway. She didn't seem happy to see him in her bedroom.

"No place I would rather be." He climbed out of bed.

"Your house isn't fixed yet?" She leaned against the doorjamb as he walked toward her.

"Doesn't matter. I still want to be here more than over there." He reached her and ran his hands over her face, kissing her lightly on the forehead. "I missed you."

"Okay," she said, her body rigid.

"How was your day?" he asked, wondering if her sisters had done or said something to upset her. Had they talked to her about him?

He didn't move any closer, just close enough to touch her, knowing that she wasn't going to be pushed. She needed to be the one to accept him being there.

"It was okay."

"Just okay? Did you have fun with your family? Did they say something about me?" He didn't want to ask but needed to know.

"No, they don't actually know about you," she admitted with a shrug.

"Are you going to tell them?" he asked, hoping she was going to tell them one day, that she wanted to tell them. He wanted to be important enough for her to tell others.

"One day, but today was not that day." The smile she gave him was small and seemed apologetic.

"When you are ready." He saw her shoulders relax as she stood in front of him.

"Thank you," she whispered, and her eyes fluttered closed.

It seemed that sleeping together hadn't changed Agatha at all. "No wounds?" He ran a finger over the scar on her forehead.

Her cheeks pinkened, and she shook her head. "No, not today. Harper's husband kept her under control. He's the only thing that controls her. She was only left with bossing me around."

"Do you listen?" he questioned, knowing she didn't like to be bossed around.

"No, not even when I'm working for her." She smiled at her admission, her body relaxing a little.

"What do you do for her?" He tucked her hair dark behind her ears, loving the silky softness of it.

"I'm a waiter for her catering company." She leaned toward him a little.

"Do you like it?" He ran his fingers down the back of her neck, which caused her to shiver slightly.

She sighed and said quietly, "No, I hate it. But I love my sisters, so I do it. How was your contractor?"

"Good, I think it'll work great. He didn't even tell me I was killing my house, unlike some noisy neighbor." He ran his fingers down her arms until he took both her hands in his.

"I can't believe Nelly is like that," she said with a chuckle, her own hands squeezing his.

"I can't either, Agatha. Who would ever do that?" Hesitantly, he started backing her toward the bed. She followed, all her hesitance gone. Just as the back of her legs hit the bed, he kissed her, and she kissed him back. His Agatha was back.

CHAPTER TWENTY-ONE

FRIDAY MORNING STARTED EARLIER than Agatha wanted it to. Just after 3 a.m., her day started with a phone call. Sera was in labor, and the girls were coming over to Agatha's. Leaving Chris sleeping, she climbed out of his warm arms and went to let the still-sleeping Emma and Violet into the house.

Since her sleep had been disturbed, she decided to draw instead of trying to sleep again. Over the last two weeks, she hadn't drawn as much as she usually did. Chris was usually there until late morning and back just after Violet left for the day. Her best time for work wasn't during the day, but her nights were now filled with Chris.

By 6 a.m., she got the call she had been waiting for, though she wouldn't admit it. Over the months, she hadn't let herself get too excited over Sera's new baby; she knew this birth wouldn't be like the other two. This baby wasn't going to be a large part of her life. Sera had Harrison, and that had changed everything. He would be there for the baby, not Agatha.

Baby boy Dean had arrived and was ready to see his sisters. Sera had wanted the girls to be a part of their new brother's life, and that including being present for the birth, but Harrison had said no. He had missed his daughter's births and was not going to share his son with anyone—even his kids, which Emma was very thankful for. Violet had been disappointed, so the baby being born as she slept was a good thing.

Agatha returned to her room to change into clothes for the day. Chris was still sleeping. He was gorgeous even in sleep. After putting on jeans and her "Pin" T-shirt, she sat down on the bed and ran her fingers through his curly hair, the strands reminded her of the eight-year-old she fell in love with.

Chris opened his eyes and squinted at her. "Morning."

"Morning. I have to get the kids ready and take them to see the new baby this morning. Sleep as long as you want." She ran her fingers through the curls one more time.

"What? Baby?" he asked in confusion.

"Harrison dropped the girls off around three. It's six now. Just sleep." Getting up, she kissed his forehead and left him to sleep the rest of the morning.

She had managed to put both girls to sleep in the same bedroom the night before—usually, Emma was against that. Being in the same room made it easier for her to wake them both with the news of their brother. Both showed more excitement than they had previously let on.

Once the kids were dressed and clean, she stopped at a fast food restaurant to get them breakfast on the way to the hospital. Once there, the little girls ran to their mom, hugged her, and took turns holding their brother. As Sera pointed out the similarities and differences the black-haired baby had with his sisters, Agatha congratulated Harrison on the boy.

"I am more excited to see the baby than anyone. All of you got to see the girls arrive. This one is my first. Thanks for being there for Sera when Violet was born. She told me you were her rock during that time." Harrison gave her a side hug.

Looking at the man, she wondered how much Sera had told him. Had she told him what happened that morning? Or just about how she took to the baby? "I didn't do anything."

"Do you want to hold the baby, Agatha?" Sera asked, looking at her closely, too closely. She was looking for weakness, something Agatha wasn't going to show.

"Not today. Later." She looked at the baby in Sera's arms, so much like Violet. The image brought that day back into sharp focus. Harrison hugged her again as if sensing her emotions, and she realized that he must know.

"Okay, we named him," Sera said, sniffing back a tear.

"Harry?" Agatha nudged Harrison away, whose arm was still around her.

"No, silly. Benjamin Lovely Dean."

"Harrison, did you let her name your kid after her ex? Didn't you just spend months changing the girls' names to Dean?" Agatha turned to the proud father, who was grinning.

Violet and Emma still maintained the Lovely last name as a second middle name. It was something that Sera had insisted, that her kids would always be Lovelys. They were a family.

"She named him after his sisters, not the ex." Harrison pointed out, refusing to let Agatha get him riled up.

"She shouldn't. Most of us aren't even Lovelys anymore."

Sera's eyes were shining with tears. "You five will always be Lovelys, even when you get married."

"You're weird." Agatha laughed at her and wiped her own tear away, but she stepped over to Sera and hugged her. Her new baby looked just like another carbon copy of his sisters.

"I'll take the girls to school since I assume more Lovelys will be here soon. You can go back home, Agatha. I hear you might have someone waiting," Harrison said not so subtly.

"Nice, Harrison. He's still sleeping."

"So not missing you?"

"Who wouldn't miss me, Harrison?" Agatha joked, not wanting to say too much, not with Sera listening and disapproving.

Without waiting for an answer, she headed out, leaving the family behind. They needed time to bond with the new arrival, and Agatha was sure Harrison wasn't in a hurry to take the girls to school.

Back at her house, she found Chris already gone from her bed. He had made it so that she didn't have to, even putting every extra pillow back on like she liked. All she wanted to do was crawl in and sleep the day away, but she decided to do something else instead.

Up in her studio, Agatha picked up the wooden box that was stored on the shelf where she kept her books. Opening the cedar box, she inhaled deeply and took out the envelope on top. The box contained at least six others, each as precious to her as the last.

Agatha pulled out the picture from the envelope of a baby in a highchair. Her entire face, hands, and bare chest were covered in long noodles and red spaghetti sauce. The baby was grinning and had dark black curls and brown eyes. And Chris's crooked smile.

Running her hand over the picture, she was filled with sadness to have missed the moment it captured, just like every moment in her life she would miss. Her baby was nine months old, and Agatha had spent less than an hour with her. She had given her up to parents that would love and care for her like Agatha couldn't at the time. The baby's new parents sent her letter after letter, letting her know how the baby was doing.

A month later, she had sold her books, but she hadn't known that would happen the morning Poppy had been born. That morning she had been at the lowest point in her life and had nothing to give a baby. Less than nothing. Her only job had been given to her by her sisters, and she wasn't even any good at it. Her dream of publishing a book was so far off she had stopped believing it would even happen. She had gotten pregnant by a man who didn't remember her eighteen months later.

Calling Chris about the baby had led her to his agent. The man had coldly told her Chris wasn't interested in her alleged baby and that if she was serious, she would demand a paternity test. Then they would discuss how much money she wanted. Hanging up, she knew she had tried to tell him, and it was now her decision, which she had already made. She couldn't keep the baby.

If Sera had been there, she would have forced Agatha to take the baby home, but Sera had just married Harrison days before and was on a honeymoon/family vacation with the two youngest girls. For months her head had been elsewhere and not focused on Agatha, who had turned more into her art as she ignored her body.

Lucy and Buzz at that point were the only ones at home, but they had not thought anything was wrong with their little sister. The others had been focused on settling into their married lives. It had been the right decision; she would not regret it now that her life was in order. The baby was with her loving parents, who wanted nothing more than to raise her as their own. They didn't care what kind of a mess Agatha was; they loved Poppy anyway.

For their part, they didn't know anything about Agatha, or they would never have named her baby Poppy, such an uplifting, fun name. Poppy would have the personality of Sera with a name like that. Nothing like Agatha.

Nine months before, she had only looked at the baby she and Chris had created. Now she was a wiggly bundle of dark hair and already had dark eyes, nothing like what she had always imagined of Jet since she had lost him. She always pictured him blond like his father. Lightly she touched the baby's cheek in the picture and knew she was better off without Agatha. Others could give her everything she deserved in life. Agatha couldn't give her anything but love, but love didn't buy diapers and clothes.

Now she could buy her everything, but she was gone. Forever just a picture of a baby who was growing up somewhere in the city, completely lost to her. Her only chance to see her was a phone number, a number she had never called.

Today she needed to make sure that her baby was where she needed to be, loved like she deserved to be loved. Pulling out her phone, she called the number for a family who never wanted to hear from her.

After the call, she tucked the picture back in the envelope and put the box back where it lived, in plain sight but hidden. She headed out of the house before she lost the nerve that seeing Benjamin had caused. She needed to see her Poppy.

CHAPTER TWENTY-TWO

THE LIVING ROOM was small and cozy, with not as many toys as Agatha would have liked the baby to have. But that didn't matter; Agatha wasn't looking at the house or the toys.

Little hands were holding on to the coffee table as she wobbled on her feet, all smiles at her accomplishment. Two little teeth showed on her wide smile. Her hair was curly and standing on end and was as black as Agatha's. The baby looked at Agatha with big brown eyes that Agatha knew were Christopher's, not her own.

"You're very good at that, Poppy." She touched her chubby arm in wonder. Her baby was amazing.

In the kitchen, both the parents were watching her and whispering to each other. Agatha knew they were worried, but there was nothing Agatha could do. The adoption was final. Though Agatha had the ability to visit the baby with her parents' consent. When she had called that morning Steven and Ronni had been more than willing to let her come for a visit.

When she had knocked on the door, the woman who answered had a blonde baby in her arms. Ronni had said the baby's name was Emma, and Agatha had told her she had a sister named Emma. Since then, Ronni had remained in the kitchen with the smaller baby until her husband had come home from work.

Taking Poppy's hand, Agatha held it so that the baby could walk away from the table, but Poppy did not trust her to not let her fall. The baby had been right to not trust her because when the chunky little legs gave out, Agatha wasn't fast enough to catch her, and she fell onto the carpeted floor. But it was enough to make Poppy cry.

When her parents didn't rush into the room, Agatha picked her up, holding her tight, wanting to make her better, wishing her baby never cried. Feeling the warm body against hers, she wanted to cry herself, not knowing how she was going to walk away from her today. This was exactly why she had never come before.

Poppy's tears subsided, and Agatha continued to hold her. She would have to give her back soon but wanted to hold her forever. Agatha cradled her head with its fine, curly hair and hoped the baby was soaking up the love Agatha was giving her.

"How is it going?" her daughter's mom asked, coming into the room.

"Good," was all Agatha could respond to the woman who was lucky enough to raise this amazing little person.

"She must know you're her mom." Ronni nodded at Poppy still in her arms.

"No, you are her mom. I won't take her away." Agatha promised, but still held her tight.

"Steven and I have been talking, and we think that you coming to see us today is a sign," Ronni said as the man came into the room.

Agatha stiffened. They were not going to let her see the girl again. It was their right to say no to her in the future; they only had to let her see Poppy when they wanted to, and if they didn't want her to, there was nothing she could do. They must have felt as awkward about her being there as Agatha did, that her being there would disrupt everything in their family. Tightening her grip on the baby she just fell in love with, she wanted to cry, right there in a stranger's living room.

"You see, Agatha, Ronni has her hands full with the two babies.

We were lucky enough to get pregnant on our own and only found out after Poppy came to us." Steven looked over to the hallway to the bedrooms.

"Emma." Poppy's baby sister, just like Agatha. They had that in common.

"Yes, Emma. And the doctors said that it happens that way sometimes. The pressure to have a baby is lessened when you adopt, and then you finally get pregnant. They don't think having more will be as difficult as having her." Ronni smiled.

"That's good. I'm from a large family. It was a great way to grow up," Agatha said, still rocking her baby, hoping the couple would let her see Poppy again, just one more time.

The couple traded glances, making Agatha's heart sink. She had only gotten to see Poppy once. It was more than she had ever thought she would want to see her, but one visit had made her realize once wasn't enough. Agatha had even taken a few pictures on her phone so that she can look at her in the future.

"What my wife means is that we will be having more children of our own. When we adopted, we thought we would never have kids of our own. Now we have Emma and will probably have more." Steven's face was serious.

"What does that mean for Poppy?" Agatha couldn't figure out what they were getting at. They loved her baby as much as she did.

"It means that we would like to back out of the adoption," Stephen said calmly, like he wanted his chicken sent back at a restaurant. Or maybe even with less caring in his voice.

"What? You don't love her?" Agatha demanded as she scrambled to her feet.

"We do love her, but we realize that we love our own daughter more," Ronni said, as if that was possible.

"You don't love her anymore? Now that you have another kid, this one is not good enough for you?" Agatha turned Poppy away from them, protecting her, not wanting her to see what was happening, even if she could hear it.

"You don't understand you don't have children," Stephen said, as if Poppy wasn't hers even if she had put her up for adoption.

"I don't need to. I am a feeling human, one who thought my kid was in a loving home. That's why I gave her up, so she could have a loving home." Agatha tried to stop the tears but couldn't.

"I have a folder containing the information your lawyer will need to get custody changed back to you." Stephen held up the file. "We already signed everything that is needed. I'm a lawyer and had it drawn up after you called. We knew it was a sign."

"You're just returning her? Like a shirt you outgrew?! My kid?" Agatha stomped over and grabbed the file from him. No way was she leaving her baby with these people.

The couple exchanged looks again and Stephen got up. "I'll get her car seat."

By the time Agatha drove away, she had enough food for a few days and a dozen diapers. Poppy was secured in the back seat of her car, and the paperwork was on the seat beside her.

Agatha drove straight to her lawyer's office. She hoped that Aspen was still there. If not, she would have to go to Harrison. This all needed to be done today. No way was she letting those two change their minds and take her baby again.

Walking into the office, she asked the receptionist for Aspen and was told she was busy this afternoon. Luckily, when Agatha broke down crying, Aspen was able to make time for her. In the same conference room she had bought her house on Monday, she watched Aspen and another lawyer looking over the paperwork in the file.

It was taking far longer for them to read the papers. She knew she should have looked at them, but her mind was full of other things. There was a long list of things she would need for the baby, and it was going to take a while to buy everything and then get it all organized. It was going to be a long day.

"It looks like everything that is needed is here. Sebastian's calling Steven and Ronni Chambers to make sure everything is done correctly. But let's get this stuff signed so when he comes back, we can just fax everything where it needs to go before the weekend." Aspen handed over the paperwork and had Agatha sign in seven places to get her daughter back.

That was all it took—less signing that she had done for her house, and she was a mother. Again.

Now she just had to tell everyone about it. Another secret she had kept from her stepmom and sisters. And what about Chris? How was she going to tell him he was a dad?

CHAPTER TWENTY-THREE

AT 3:10 P.M., Chris saw Violet sitting on the front step of Agatha's house. The house had been quiet all day. He hadn't seen Agatha except when she had woken him to tell him she was leaving with the girls. Now she was ten minutes late to meet Violet, and it looked like Violet had already checked around the house.

Jogging over to her, he asked, "No Agatha?"

Violet was on the verge of tears. "No, I can't find her in the house, and her car is gone. I think she forgot me."

"She would not forget about you. She must have got caught in traffic or something. Can I sit with you?"

"Yes. She doesn't have cookies out." Violet got up and walked into the house. Agatha always had cookies out for Violet when she got home from school. Just like the pop and mail, it was a ritual.

Chris wondered where Agatha could be. For the first time, he started to worry that she had been in an accident or something. No way would she miss Violet coming home from school.

"Where is Emma?" he asked.

"A friend's house," Violet said and rolled her eyes. "A new friend Mom thinks is a nice girl but isn't."

"Do you know where the cookies are?" He followed her through the kitchen.

"In the freezer. Lucy makes them for Agatha." The girl went into the freezer and pulled out a bag of four cookies.

Both he and Violet looked at the frozen peanut butter cookies. It said "B Ratt" on the bag, making Chris chuckle, but not Violet. Lucy was the one behind the shirts.

He poked at the frozen dessert. "We'll have to wait a few minutes."

"Okay. I'll check the studio one more time," Violet said and was gone. After a moment, she was back with a sad face, no Agatha up there.

Chris had no idea where a studio would be in the house, but he hadn't been in every room yet. Agatha was still nervous that he would break her house and always kept an eye on him. He hadn't broken anything in over a week at his house, mostly because he was not allowed to do much. Others were fixing it now, and he had to admit he was no handyman.

"Are you going to see the baby again today?" Chris asked her in hopes of making her happy. Today was the first time he had seen the little girl sad since she had complained that Nick J. had called her sparkly.

"Yes. Buzzy will pick us up and bring us to the hospital again." She didn't sound happy about it.

"Did you see the baby this morning?" Chris asked, knowing she had.

"Yes, and I got to hold him, but Agatha didn't." She opened the bag of cookies.

"Did she say where she was going today?" Chris realized he was questioning a little girl about his girlfriend. Was she his girlfriend? They hadn't talked about it, but he wanted to, soon.

"No, she didn't say anything." The little girl's eyes swept the house again, like she still couldn't believe that Agatha wasn't there. "Do you think she's coming back?"

"Of course she's coming back; she lives here. Why would she not come home? Has she ever not come home before?" he asked as she kicked the counter lightly with her toes.

"No, but she's always here. She always works when I'm asleep or at least when Mom is here," Violet said.

"She'll be here tomorrow. I promise." He hoped it was a promise he could keep because he hated that Violet was sad. "What did they name the baby?"

"Benjamin Lovely. Mom named him, like Emmaline." She was still kicking the counter and he let her. She deserved to do what she wanted today.

"But not you?"

She grinned. "Nope, Agatha named me."

"After a pretty flower." He handed her another cookie.

"Nope, after the color. I'm an artist. Sometimes Agatha doesn't see me, and she calls me ultraviolet." She giggled.

"Agatha loves colors." He had noticed it over the last few weeks. When she described something, it wasn't red, it was auburn or brick or burgundy. His blue shirt had been azure, and his green shirt had been Turkish blue, not green.

"Her favorite is walnut brown. One year for her birthday, I bought her a pencil in that color. It's her favorite," Violet explained.

"Do you want to watch cartoons and find the mistakes?" he asked, not knowing what else to do with her. The only thing they had in common was Agatha, and she was missing.

"Sure, until Buzz comes. Since Mom and Dad are at the hospital still, I am going to her house for the night." She climbed off the stool.

It was a little after 5 p.m. when a redhead came in the door without knocking. Violet was off the couch and ran to her sister, yelling her name. After a quick hug, the redhead looked him over and asked, "Where's Agatha?"

"I don't know. I found Violet on the step at 3 p.m., and we haven't heard from Agatha," he said.

"I'm Bea. Agatha doesn't leave the house much unless she's working, but she wouldn't work during the day. She's a vampire, isn't she, Violet?"

"She is not. She goes out in the sun!" the girl argued with a giggle. It seemed like an ongoing joke.

"Chris Lowell," he put out his hand, which she ignored.

"I know who you are. Don't hurt her." Her brown eyes held his.

"I won't," He stated.

"Agatha puts on this air that nothing touches her, and not much does. But when she gets hurt, it takes her a long time to recover. Sometimes she doesn't. She isn't some plaything," Bea warned. She was no taller than her sister, but she was willing to stand up to him for her.

"She's not," he agreed.

With her dark eyes still on him, she pulled out her phone and pushed some buttons. Her eyes squinted as it rolled to voicemail, and Bea dialed anther number.

"Luce, have you talked to Ag today?" She turned her back on him as she spoke. "No, she wasn't here when Violet came home. I'm picking up Violet."

As she talked, she walked out the door, leaving him to wonder if any of her sisters knew where she was.

Without knowing what else to do, he went across the street to see what the crew had finished since he had spent the afternoon with Violet. The walls were sheetrocked and were now ready for paint, and the tile in the kitchen and bathrooms was done. All the bathrooms and kitchen were in working order. The house wasn't going to be a master-piece of original workmanship because he had destroyed most of that, but his contractor had told him that modern design in old houses was all the rage, so they had changed direction and started over. It would still be a nice house, just different than he had originally dreamed.

Deciding it was safe for him to pick up garbage around the house, he filled a bag of bottles and cans from beverages and odds and ends that could be thrown out. He knew the house was still half done, but in a few more weeks, he either had to live in it or sell it. When he began the project, he had planned to sell it and move on to another project, but now he knew there would be no other project. And he didn't want to live there either. He was happier across the street with Agatha.

Her prickly side rarely came out anymore, and when it did, it was because she was trying to protect herself from something. Earlier in the week, she yelled at him all day on Monday before he left for work, but when he came home, she was in a better mood.

Before he knew it, an hour had passed, so he went and checked to see if her car was back. Grinning, he saw it was sitting right where it always did in the yard. Why she parked on the grass, he didn't know. Shutting off lights and locking the door, he headed across the street. On the porch there was a box sitting by the door. Glancing at it, he saw his Turkish blue shirt on top. He tried to open the door but found that it was locked.

Agatha had been gone all day, and now she had kicked him out of her house. No explanation, nothing. He had no idea what he had done. Should he have gone with her to the hospital that morning? It had been a family event, and she hadn't invited him. He was beginning to believe he needed to start inviting himself.

Chris decided he needed an explanation and began pounding on the door. He yelled her name, knowing she was in there and that she could hear him.

She opened the door a crack and looked out it. "Stop being so loud, Chris."

"What is this?" He pointed to the box.

"Your stuff. We're done," she stated calmly.

"Why? Where were you today?" he demanded.

"It doesn't concern you."

"What? I was the one who sat with the saddest nine-year-old in the state for two hours, who kept asking if you were ever coming back!" He hoped she would understand how sad Violet had been. Though he was sure she knew, he wanted her to feel guilty about it.

She didn't open the door any wider. "I just can't do this right now."

"What did I do?"

"Nothing, Chris, it's me. This was never going anywhere. It needs to be over now."

"Over now, Agatha? I have no say in it?"

"No, Christopher. This is my life. You don't even know me!" She yelled and tried to shut the door on him.

"Because you don't let me, Agatha." He pushed the door open and saw the entire living room was full of cardboard, plastic, and plastic bags. The couch was covered in pink clothes and baby toys.

"Get out, Chris. Get out of my house and my life. I don't need you. I have never needed you." She pushed against his chest to push him from the house, but she had no hopes of moving him. They both knew that.

"Stop it, Agatha." His arms pulled her to him. He held her tight as she pushed and twisted to get free and cried. Tightening his hold on her, he kicked the door closed behind them. Whatever had happened that day had been hard on her, and what he had learned since meeting her was that when her emotions ran high, she pushed people away. Anger was her go-to emotion.

Looking around the room more closely, he saw a playpen amongst the mess, and a baby was peeking over the side, looking at him. Only the baby's black curly hair and dark eyes were visible, along with two tiny hands holding on to the top of the playpen.

"Agatha, there's a baby here," he whispered to her, not taking his eyes from it. In his arms, she stiffened and pushed away from him again, but he tightened his arms around her. "She's staring at me. I think she might be dangerous."

After feeling her laugh at his joke, he relaxed his hold a tiny bit. The baby seemed content, so he kept holding Agatha. Agatha needed holding right now. Whatever she had been doing had brought a baby into her house.

"I have to get this all cleaned up," she said into his chest.

"I will clean it up. You do whatever needs to be done with the baby." He ran a hand over her hair before releasing her.

"Poppy, her name is Poppy." She walked over and picked up the baby from the playpen. Poppy was in tiny pink footie pajamas with a duck on them.

"Hi, Poppy. I'm Chris." He gently took the girl's hand and shook it.

Knowing something was up with Agatha, Chis started to clean the living room. He found a garbage bag and filled it with plastic and cardboard. There were more bags of stuff on the floor that she hadn't even opened yet. At this point, he was not going to ask questions in case she tried to toss him out again. He didn't want her to be alone.

Once the second bag was full, he glanced at Agatha on the couch and was only met by one set of brown eyes, the others were closed in sleep. With a smile, he slid the wide-awake little girl from her arms. For her part, Poppy didn't cry or seem nervous that a stranger was holding her. She just smiled at him with her two little teeth.

Over the years, Chris had never spent time with any kids, even his sister's kids. When they had been this young, he had been thinking about nothing but football. It seemed he had missed a lot for his football dreams—dreams that didn't even feel real anymore. It had only been a year, and he was already over those dreams.

Setting Poppy in her playpen, he carefully carried Agatha up to her bedroom. She must have been exhausted because she didn't even stir. Once she was in bed, he turned his attention to the baby again. Taking her out of the playpen, he sat her on his lap and worked through her bags, opening packages of pink clothes and little toys that Poppy inspected with interest as he went.

Once again, he cleaned the floor after filling another bag with garbage and wondered what to do with all the stuff. He asked Poppy but only got a smile in return. The only thing he was sure of was that Agatha was all in with this baby. Poppy was here to stay.

Two giant boxes of diapers didn't say weekend visit, nor did hundreds of dollars' worth of clothes and toys. With the baby in his arms, he decided some stuff could be put away; he just needed a place to put it. With his empty arm, he carried the tan highchair to the kitchen, deciding to put it by the island.

There was a manila folder on the mostly empty counter, like the one she had been looking at weeks before when she had been so prickly. Was it about the baby girl or something else?

Flipping it open, he saw adoption papers, signed by a judge and none other than Agatha C. Lovely for a Poppy Joy Chambers. They were dated today. Chris sat down and stared at the papers. He couldn't really believe it. He had woken up beside her this morning, or would have if she hadn't woken up first, and she hadn't said anything. Nor over the last three weeks he had known her. She had to have known. She had to have been working on it.

Did she think he would disapprove and tell her not to do it? What *would* he have said? At this point, he didn't know, but he knew she thought he would be mad. That's why she tried to end it; because she thought he wouldn't be happy with her having a child.

Looking at the curly black hair, he knew he had to prove himself, because this child was hers now. If he wanted Agatha, he had to accept this little one and any others she might bring home. And he wanted Agatha.

Also in the folder was a hand-printed list of when things needed to be done. Poppy was going to need to be fed soon based on the sheet. He was not going to fail at this.

An hour later, he had Poppy's diaper changed, made and fed her a bottle, and she was fast asleep in his arms. But he had no idea what to do with the baby now. As far as he knew, she had no crib in the house, and the playpen was miles from Agatha's bedroom upstairs.

He checked all the other rooms to see if she had actually put up a crib while he was gone or even days before in preparation but found nothing. All the rooms looked like the one he had stayed in, just different color schemes and layouts. All rooms had a queen-sized bed and a dresser. Some had stuff on the walls, some didn't. He didn't see how six grown women and two kids had lived in the house at the same time. There were only eight bedrooms, and that included the master. He was tempted to check the attic for a crib but figured she would have hauled it down already if she had one. With that, he gave up on finding a crib.

After a few false starts, he silently got the playpen up to Agatha's bedroom. Then he took the baby and put her in the playpen and covered her with a pink blanket.

Downstairs, he tossed the bags out the back door to be dealt with later and organized the living room a little more so that it didn't look like a pink bomb had gone off in it. Life was going to be different here tomorrow. No more sleeping in and having sex when he wanted her.

Agatha was a parent now. And he hoped that she would let him help her. He wanted to do this with her.

CHAPTER TWENTY-FOUR

A BUZZING PHONE woke Agatha earlier than she usually liked. Ignoring it, she snuggled deeper into the covers. She could feel the rough fabric encasing her legs and wondered why she was wearing jeans in bed.

Pulling out the phone, she answered it with a sleepy, "Morning."

"Where the hell have you been?" Sera yelled at her. Sera never yelled.

"Home, sleeping." Rolling over, she realized Chris wasn't with her. She missed him right away.

"Bull. You weren't home when Violet came home from school yesterday." Sera was pissed, which was not a normal emotion for the woman. That meant that Agatha was in trouble.

Sitting up Agatha, dropped the phone. Suddenly, she was reminded of the events of the day before. From Sera's baby's birth to bringing Poppy home with her. The baby wasn't in the room with her, and she had no idea where she was. A glance at the clock told her she had been sleeping for twelve hours. She had been right. She wasn't mother material. She had lost her baby in less than one day!

Scrambling out of bed, Agatha left the phone where it had dropped and was almost to the door when Chris came into the room holding

Poppy in his arms. He was shirtless, and she was resting her head on his shoulder, her little chunky hand lying on his chest.

Relief turned into pain as she saw them together. Her daughter in the arms of the man she loved—their daughter. Both appeared content and happy with the situation. It seemed Chris had taken over the duties of parenting without her asking; in fact, she had told him not to, but here he was, melting her heart in just another way.

Agatha grabbed the phone off the floor when she realized Sera was still yelling her name. "Sorry, Sera, I just had something big come up yesterday and it took way longer than I thought it would. How's the baby?"

Sera sighed and started to tell her all the things Benjamin had mastered in his first day of life, from eating every two hours without fail to latching on almost immediately. They were even getting out of the hospital a day early because the baby was so smart, or so Sera said. Her anger was forgotten, at least for a moment. Agatha listened as Chris sat down on the bed with Poppy still in his arms. Exactly where Agatha wanted to be.

"When you get out of the hospital, we can talk then," Agatha said, knowing Sera had two more days in the hospital. And knowing Sera's anger at Agatha would be tiny compared to her finding out Agatha had put a baby up for adoption without her even knowing.

"Yes, we will," Sera said as if she knew everything that was going on and was not pleased. The woman probably thought that her being gone had something to do with Chris.

Hanging up on her stepmother, Agatha asked, "How's Poppy? I'm sorry I crashed. I shouldn't have. I'm responsible for her now; I can't just sleep when I need to anymore."

"We did just fine. There were a few rocky moments, but we made it through. Poppy's not sure she loves pink," he joked, trying to ease her worries.

"She has no choice. The baby industry says she loves it. I got other clothes in other colors when I could find them." She touched the baby's back, wanting to take her away from Chris but also wanting to enjoy watching him hold their baby for just for a moment longer.

"Does your mom know about her?" he asked.

Biting her lip, Agatha pushed herself up against the headboard. "No, I never told her. She was in the middle of a pretty hot affair at the time and didn't notice."

"She had an affair while she was dating Harrison?" he asked in surprise.

"The affair was *with* Harrison. Then she was busy with marriage prep and planning all my sisters' weddings. We hosted quite a few weddings this last year. Nobody was paying much attention to me, and I just wanted them happy and not to worry about anything," she admitted. Even if she wouldn't have it any other way, it still made her sad.

"That doesn't explain whose baby Poppy is," he pushed, rubbing the baby's back.

Agatha took a deep breath. "Mine. I gave her up for adoption when she was born. Yesterday, her parents gave her back. Apparently, they have a new baby they like more." She drew up her knees and watched him. Even now, she couldn't see that she'd had any other choice. How could she not have taken her baby back?

"What the hell? Who could not love Poppy best?" He hugged Poppy to him, just like Agatha had the day before. He wanted to protect her from the world also.

"The couple had one of their own last month." She gently pulled the baby from his arms and held her tight, needing to hold her close.

He grabbed Agatha's foot and rubbed it with his thumb, then asked quietly, "You don't have to answer, but why did you feel like you had to give her up in the first place?"

Looking at her daughter's curls, she felt the misery she went through when she did it again. Agatha closed her eyes. "I wasn't doing so great at life then. Everyone still lived here at the house, and I was able to hide from the world. I do that sometimes. I had quit or been fired from all my jobs, and nothing was working out in my life. I was doing worse than a high schooler—at least they thought they had a future. I didn't. Then I was got stupidly pregnant. Nobody else got pregnant; well, Lucy did, but I didn't know that at the time."

It had only been after Poppy was long gone that both her sisters, Lucy and Buzz, had gotten pregnant before getting married. In both cases, everyone rallied around the new mothers, which made Agatha realize she should have just said something from the start. But it was too late, and for both of her sisters, the babies' dads had been in love with their mothers. All were now happily married. That wasn't going to happen for her. No matter what her heart wanted, her brain knew better.

"You were not stupid, Agatha. It happens." Chris tried to comfort her.

"Yeah. I do stupid stuff all the time. I gave Poppy away to people who were supposed to love her forever no matter what. But no, they ended up just like my parents and wanted out when something better came along. Everybody leaves." She hugged the baby to her, hating that Poppy had felt the pain of rejection even for a moment. But hopefully, she was too young to remember later—unlike Agatha.

"When are you going to tell your mom? You can't hide Poppy for long. Nobody even knocks when they come in the house," Chris reminded her.

"I have to wait until she comes home from the hospital. Let her and Benjamin have their time without me getting in the way," Agatha replied, though she knew she was only stalling for time.

"I don't think she'll mind. I think she'll be pretty excited to meet Poppy."

"She's going to be pissed."

"How did you carry and give birth to a baby in a house full of people?"

"Nobody was paying much attention to me. They cared that I was gaining weight, but nobody said anything. And then Poppy was born while Sera and her new family were all on vacation. It worked out perfectly, actually. Harper and Maby were married and didn't live here anymore. Lucy was staying with Maby that week. Buzz was around but was working, and I just told her I was with friends. Nobody ever questioned it." At the time, she thought luck was finally turning her way, oddly only so that she could give away the one thing she loved more than life itself. All without anyone knowing it had happened.

"Until yesterday. Then it wasn't so perfect. Or maybe that means it is perfect because your life is back on track, and you can raise her now," he said, moving closer to Agatha and tucking her hair behind her ear.

"But I fell asleep and didn't know where she was." Agatha knew she had messed up badly. It was way too soon for her to feel that it was going to be alright.

"I knew. You were tired, Agatha. When I'm here, I will help you." He kissed her lips above the baby's head.

"But she's mine. I need to take care of her all the time."

Because there was one thing she knew: she couldn't count on Chris being there for her all the time. He didn't even know her; not really. And once he did, he would be gone. Because nobody stuck around for Agatha Christie Lovely ... they never had. Why would Chris be any different?

CHAPTER TWENTY-FIVE

THE WEEKEND BLEW by with Agatha's every thought and move centered around a nine-month-old baby. Saturday, Chris left most of the baby care to Agatha because after their talk, he knew she needed to prove to herself that she could do it. She had convinced herself that she couldn't be a mother, and the only way for her to realize she was going to be fine was for her to do a lot of it alone.

So around noon on Saturday, he had went out to buy the crib she hadn't been able to fit in her car the day before. While in the store, he bought a few more things that the saleswoman had insisted would make his life easier—their lives easier. On his way out of the store, he saw them: Christie Lovely's books. Buying two of the six available, he was excited about his find. He had completely forgotten about the books until that moment. So much had changed in his life since he had found out about his former locker neighbor's books.

After he got home, he put up the crib, which involved removing the bed from the room across from the master bedroom. With no place to put the old mattress, he dragged it to the basement after Agatha told him not to put it in the attic.

By the time Poppy was sleeping in her new bedroom, Chris was just as exhausted and went to bed too. Agatha stayed up to clean and organize the house a little. He suspected she needed a little alone time also.

When she climbed into bed a few hours later, she tried not to wake him, but he was alerted to her movements and pulled her into his arms. He wanted her to know that he was still interested in her, that he still wanted her.

Sunday had been a bit more relaxed, with both knowing what to expect from the day. No trips to the store were needed, and they had spent most of the day on the floor with Poppy, trying to make up for the nine months she had been with parents that might not have loved her like they should have.

Over the weekend, Agatha had spoken to most of her sisters but hadn't said anything about him or Poppy. She let her sisters dictate the conversation, which was mostly questions about why she'd been missing that day. He wondered if she had received the same calls when she had been alone, having a baby. Had they called only to yell at her that time as well?

On Monday, he went over to his house but felt he was only in the way of the workers and wanted to be home with Agatha and Poppy again. So he did, leaving at noon. It wasn't like he was any help anyway.

The house was silent when he arrive,d and he couldn't find Agatha or the baby anywhere. The first floor was empty, and the second floor was empty also. Bedrooms were quiet, but there was faint music coming from above his head. Deciding to investigate, he walked down to the attic door, and when he opened it, Bon Jovi was playing quietly from the floor above.

He silently walked up the stairs until Agatha sitting at an easel with Poppy on her lap came into view. Agatha was holding the baby's hand over a pencil and was drawing on a white piece of paper.

"See, Poppy? You can draw too. This is magenta. It's a darker pink than your shirt. Your shirt is called bubblegum, like this pencil. People always just call it pink, but we know better." She kissed Poppy's black hair.

Tearing his eyes from the woman, he took in the rest of the room, which contained a bed and a couch. But the easel took center stage, and the storage of art supplies off to the side was massive. This room was Agatha's; everything in the room screamed this was Agatha's. This must have been her room, her sanctuary when everyone still lived at home.

It hurt him that for as long as he had been sleeping in her bed, she hadn't felt like she could share this space with him. That she didn't think he would want to know every part of her, even this one.

Her soft voice brought his attention back to the woman. Suddenly, he wanted to prove to her that there wasn't a part of her he didn't find fascinating. He knew it would start with this, today.

"See, you make a circle like this." Agatha still held the baby's chunky hand. "Then another circle here and here and some lines, and then you have a mouse. Usually, you don't draw the mouse in magenta, but today is for learning."

"Did you teach Violet to draw this young?"

Agatha jumped in her chair and slowly turn to him. Quickly she looked around her room and then back at him. He hated that she thought she had to hide this from him. He knew every inch of her body, but this, she didn't want to share with him.

"No, she was younger. Sera held her so much the first few months that Violet cried when she wasn't held, so I had to draw while holding her." Shrugging, she pried the pencil from Poppy's hand, then set it down in a holder on the corner of the easel.

Instantly, he regretted saying anything and not leaving immediately to let her have her space. "Don't stop because of me, Agatha. Don't be ashamed of who you are."

"I have been made fun of all my life for being artsy," she admitted, holding the baby between them, as if she needed a barrier.

"I should have realized you were an artist. Violet got her snarky cartoon watching from you. You never just say blue or brown; you always have a specific name for each color. Violet said your favorite color was walnut." He grinned when her eyes darted to the cup holding her colored pencils.

"It usually is, but sometimes it's winter white." Agatha bit her lip as if she had said too much. He hated the reaction, hated everyone who had made fun of her for any reason.

"Can I come up?" He hadn't moved from the top of the stairs.

Looking around the room again, she didn't meet his eyes. "If you want. Not much to see up here."

"I don't think so. You had the biggest room in the house and gave it up for the master bedroom?"

"This doesn't have a bathroom, and I was wasting an entire floor."

Walking over to her, he took the baby and pulled Agatha into his arms and kissed her. Looking into her eyes, he said, "Your kid drew a pretty nice mouse, Agatha. She gets that from you."

When he kissed her again, Poppy started to squirm in his arms. "I'll take her down and let you work. Come down when you feel like it. We'll be okay."

"No, I'll come down. I shouldn't be up here anyway. There's so much to do." Agatha started to pick up the scattered colored pencils.

"I will do it. You keep working. Be happy, Agatha." He kissed her forehead and headed down the stairs, knowing she needed her time in her studio to herself, though he hoped that she was willing to be herself with him also.

On the main floor, he smiled and wondered if that was where she had been when her song timer had gone off the other day. Did she always come down the stairs singing and happy? He knew she must.

Sitting on the floor with Poppy, Chris held her hands so that she could wobble stand—she liked to do that. Even today, she was less wobbly and would try to take steps, usually twisting and falling to the ground in her attempt. Her tiny green pants were topped with a once-white shirt. Now it had odd, multicolored stains from lunch.

Looking at Agatha's daughter, he could already see her in the baby's eyes and nose. Their shared dark coloring was the most obvious, but she already had her cautious yet easy laugh that was all Agatha. In just three days, he knew that.

Poppy was giggling as she tried to crawl away from him. She had mastered crawling and was quick when she wanted to be. Suddenly, the door opened, and a blonde carrying a car seat walked into the house and stopped when she saw him.

He knew immediately that it was Sera, Agatha's stepmom. Even if he had only seen her once, the baby seat in her arms was a dead giveaway.

"*You*," she said without enthusiasm as she looked him over before her eyes landed on Poppy. Though she nearly smiled at the baby, she stopped herself and frowned at them both.

"Hi, I'm Chris Lowell," he said, but he figured she already knew who he was by her greeting.

"Yes, I know. I'm Sera Dean, Agatha's mother." The woman wasn't even ten years older than Agatha. But after knowing Agatha for as long as he had, he knew Agatha also felt like Sera was her mother, no matter her age.

"Agatha's upstairs, drawing."

"I don't like this. I just want you to know that I do not like you or what you have done to her. She deserves so much better than you." With that, she took her baby and left the room, heading for the stairs, ignoring Poppy as she went. Poppy, though, watched the woman with sudden attention.

Chris watched her go and wondered what he had done to Agatha that made this woman hate him already. What had Agatha told her? Nothing came to mind as Poppy got away from him as she tried to catch up with the woman, who wasn't a fan of either of them.

It bothered him that she didn't like him. Over the years, many people had disliked him, but none had been important to Agatha. Not one that could change Agatha's mind about him, and that was what worried him the most. Losing her.

With Poppy back in his arms, he wondered how the conversation was going upstairs. Was Sera going to be as mad as Agatha thought that she was going to be? Or would she be happy to have Poppy in the family? He hoped it was the latter. Agatha already felt bad enough about the entire situation.

CHAPTER TWENTY-SIX

AFTER CHRIS HAD TAKEN Poppy downstairs, Agatha had turned her full concentration to her drawing. Humming along with Bon Jovi, Agatha switched to a lighter brown for the underside of the deer's belly. Today she needed to get back to drawing. It had been days since she had put in any time at her studio. She hadn't been able to devote as much time to her work as she would have liked.

Before she ventured into the attic with Poppy, she had sent a text to Harper and Lucy letting them know that she would not be able to work this week. No excuse, just that she couldn't do it. So far, they hadn't gotten back to her. They must have both been busy.

Footsteps on the stairs made her look up to see what Chris wanted. He had taken to the baby as much as she had this past weekend. She hated that she hadn't told him he was the father, but he could be gone at any moment. They had no future plans; they were just having fun, after all.

The blonde head that appeared instead of Chris made Agatha stifle a groan. It was Sera, who would have been pissed to see Chris. And there was no telling what she would say about Poppy.

"Afternoon, Ag. I thought Benji and I would come over and visit.

Maybe we should have called?" She set the carrier down, the tiny baby sleeping.

"Hi, Mom."

Sera sat in the old green chair she always used when they talked.

"I don't want to be the kind of a mom who pries in her kid's lives. I should be since your lives are fascinating, but I try not to." Sera took a deep breath. "But Christopher Lowell is in your living room with a baby right now, and I have no idea how that happened."

"I've been letting Chris stay with me for a few weeks," Agatha explained, not bothering to mention exactly where he was staying. The last that Sera had heard, he was staying in Mabel's room. Agatha hoped that Sera would still believe that.

"I knew that. Violet talks about him all the time. And he was here on Friday when Violet was alone. Do you know what you're doing, Agatha?" Sera leaned back in the chair.

"Yes and no. He doesn't know who I am," she admitted to her best friend. "He doesn't know I'm Christie."

"How can he not? You've barely changed since then." As their mom, Sera had a hard time seeing that her kids were getting older.

"I don't know. I thought he would realize it right away, but he never did. But he likes me as I am now." She put her pencil down, knowing she wouldn't be getting back to what she was doing for a while. There was a lecture coming.

"You've always had a hard time letting people see you as you are, Ag. People can't like what they don't see." Sera tapped Agatha's knee with her foot. "It's always been him, Ag, always. What happens when he leaves again? I was there last time. I have never been so worried about any of my kids as I was then. You didn't leave this room that summer, and I didn't think you would go to college. Luckily you went, but then you quit right away. Violet was the only reason you came back to us."

Looking back on that time, she knew Sera was right; she had let her emotions take over her life for a long time. As time has passed, she liked to think nobody noticed, but Sera did.

"I don't know what the future is going to be. I'm trying to live in the now," Agatha replied, hoping her voice sounded more confident than she actually felt. Though she wanted forever with him, she knew she was never getting that. Not with Chris.

Because no matter how much time they spent together, it was just an extended version of the other times they had been together. Once the real world intruded, he would forget all about her and go on with his life. Without her.

"So you love him, and now he's making you fall for his kid? I assume it's his kid. All her stuff is down there." Sera's blue eyes stared at her.

Agatha realized just how much of Poppy's stuff had taken over the house in just a short amount of time. There was no hiding her from anyone who walked in the door.

"Actually, no. She's mine." Agatha ripped the Band-Aid off. She had to tell them sometime. Putting off telling Sera about what was happening in her life hadn't worked well lately.

Sera laughed as if she'd told her a joke. Agatha did not join in, just leaned back in her chair as she bit her lower lip and watched her mom slowly stop laughing. Once she stopped, Agatha shrugged, and Sera swore viciously before stomping back down the stairs.

Sera was back in moments, carrying Poppy, who was looking at her new grandma with the same happy inspection she met everyone with. Sera sat back in the chair and stared at the baby, then at Agatha, and then at the baby again.

"Where the fuck was I?" Sera demanded in anger, only to smile when Poppy smiled at her.

"Hawaii with the kids and Harrison. I put her up for adoption. I couldn't raise her then."

Sera touched Poppy's cheek. "What changed?"

"I sold my books the next month. If I had sold them sooner, I could have kept her, but I had nothing and no way to earn anything. I worked as a bartender and was bad at it. Waitressing for my sisters? That doesn't buy diapers, lunches in school, or college. I couldn't keep her. It was just like when I was nineteen, except this time I didn't lose the baby. But I was in the same place, only older, and I no longer had dreams of being anything. I wasn't enough." She let the tears leak from her eyes.

"You had us." Sera began crying too.

"I didn't want to be that kind of mom. When we helped you raise the girls, you were in college trying to better yourself, and then you had a good job. I couldn't do that. I thought it was better this way." Agatha couldn't say more. There was nothing left to say.

"You know we always loved you, Agatha, no matter what you did or didn't do. We loved you through it all." Sera hugged the baby, knowing that Agatha wouldn't want the hug her mom so wanted to give. "What happened? How did you get her back?"

"After Benji was born, I just had to see her. I could since it was an open adoption. I went over there and played with her for a few hours. Turns out her parents had been able to conceive naturally after they adopted Poppy and didn't want a baby that wasn't theirs anymore. They didn't want her and gave her back to me." Agatha wiped her face dry with her shirt.

"That is not how it works. Once you adopt, they are yours forever. I'll have Harrison make sure they never get a chance to see our baby again. Papers will need to be filed," Sera said, pulling out her phone with one hand, the other still holding Poppy.

Agatha took her phone from her hand. "I went straight to Aspen, my lawyer, on Friday. It's all taken care of. You had just had a baby, so I didn't want to bother you. Aspen knew a judge and got everything done that day. That's why I wasn't there for Violet."

"Why didn't you tell me?" Sera wiped away her tears and hugged the baby to her.

"I ruined Violet's birthday. I didn't want to ruin Benji's too! I wonder if I did something shitty on Emma's?" Agatha said.

"I don't remember, but what happened on the day Violet was born didn't ruin anything. You losing your own baby made having her that much more precious. Yeah, it's sad, but that day we didn't walk out of the hospital empty-handed; we came home with a baby we have shared ever since. And now we're mothers again. I have one, and you have one. But they still look the same." Sera grinned and ran her hand over the baby's head.

"I never looked at it like that," Agatha admitted. She'd never managed to see a positive from the babies being born on the same day. Just the shadow it had cast on Violet's birth.

"How old is she? No wait, I was on my honeymoon so, just over nine months?"

"January third," Agatha confirmed. The best and worst day of her life.

Running her hand over the baby's hair again, Sera asked, "Does Chris know he is the father?"

Shocked, Agatha stammered, "W-what? How did you know?"

"The curls, his smile, and the fact that he was at a football party the girl's catered around the time you would have gotten pregnant. A party you worked." Sera turned the baby so that Agatha could see her, as if she needed to see her to know the truth.

It was something she hated herself for hiding but couldn't bring herself to tell him. Because then he would hate her also.

"No, he doesn't. He doesn't remember me. Then or before. I don't think he'll be happy when he finds out," she admitted, which was why she wasn't telling him. Maybe he never needed to know. Maybe it would never come up.

"He might be okay with it. She's a cute baby. She looks a lot like my favorite daughter. What's her name?" Sera asked.

"Poppy Joy. I have to get her name changed to Lovely. Maybe Harrison can handle that since you've done it twice over the last year for your girls." Agatha took her baby from her mom.

"She does look like a Poppy, though," Sera said and laughed. "Can I tell everyone about her? I want to tell everyone."

"I wasn't looking forward to that at all. You tell them and explain everything. Just not the Chris stuff." Her family didn't have to know everything.

"There are some things you have to explain yourself. But first, you have to tell Chris. From what I saw, he might not be so against being a dad," Sera stated.

Agatha hugged Poppy. "I don't know."

But she knew her mom was right. Chris needed to know. He needed to know everything. Only then could he decide if he really wanted to be there.

"Now I have to tell all my girls. Oh, and come over around 6 p.m. for supper. I'm sure Lucy and Harper can whip something up by then. Besides, all the girls will want to meet their new niece. And I need to spoil her! I've missed so much time with her." Sera got up and hugged them both, grabbed her baby still sleeping in his seat, and headed down the stairs.

Now everyone would know about her biggest secret. Hopefully, they would be as happy about Poppy as had been about her last secret.

CHAPTER TWENTY-SEVEN

CHRIS HELD Agatha's daughter as they walked to her mom's house at the end of the block. The baby was helping to calm his nerves. He didn't even know why he was nervous, except for the fact that they might all hate him like Sera did. Taking Agatha's hand, he squeezed it because she was probably even more nervous than he was.

Agatha's mom had left the house without saying a word or even looking at him. She had left with an anger he didn't think Violet's mom could possess—an anger that he was sure was directed at him.

When Agatha had made it down the stairs, she had said they were going to her mom's for supper and that everyone knew about him and the baby and the entire story. Which might be more then he knew because he hadn't pushed her for more information about the baby, and she wasn't saying anything.

Which meant he had no idea what he was walking into. But to be there for Agatha, he would walk through that door every day of the week.

Walking up the steps, he noticed Violet on an old wooden swing, watching them walk up. "Is that her?" she asked.

Chris decided to let Agatha handle it.

"Yes, Violet. This is Poppy."

Violet walked over to them and looked at the baby. "She doesn't look red."

"What color does she look like?" Agatha asked.

"More purple," Violet said, still frowning.

"No, she doesn't. Do you like the name?" Agatha took Poppy from his arms.

"I guess since it is a color. Benji isn't a color." The baby grabbed Violet's hand as if to shake it, causing Violet to finally smile.

"I think I like it too. To be honest, at first, I didn't. It seemed too happy and vibrant for my daughter, but I'm hoping she's like you and Mom. All bubbly." Agatha tickled the girl.

Chris looked at Agatha and realized they had never talked about her daughter's name or that she hadn't felt it was fitting for her child. Except Chris knew it was. When Agatha let down her guard, she was just as happy and bubbly as her sister. The prickly, angry woman was just a facade she hid behind.

"I'm not bubbly," Violet said as she giggled.

"You're just as bubbly as your mom. I love that about you. Is everyone here?" Agatha looked in the front window, worry back on her face.

"Yes, they were early and were talking about you. I left." Violet shrugged.

"I should go in there, shouldn't I?" Agatha asked the girl, as if she was hoping the nine-year-old would tell her to run home.

"Yes, I will stay out here, though," Violet said.

"I'll stay with Violet," Chris said, not wanting Agatha to keep stressing about her sisters. He didn't want to be the reason for more tension between them. Let them fall in love with Poppy, then he could go in.

"Okay." Agatha took a deep breath before getting up and taking the baby with her inside.

When the door shut, Chris looked at the little girl and said, "On Friday, you said you wanted a girl cousin, and now you have one."

"I know, and I thought I would be more excited, but I'm not. Mom told me after school today. Right there." She pointed to the stoop as if she would remember the moment forever.

"On the step, like how Agatha waits for you?" Chris questioned.

"She should have told me inside. Not outside," Violet said in anger.

"Why not outside?" he asked in confusion.

"Because when I walk alone from the bus, my friend walks with me, and he heard." She bit her lip.

Chris didn't understand why Violet was upset. "I don't think your friend will care that you have a new cousin."

"No, he does. Nobody can see him," Violet confided.

"Have you always known him?" Chris realized that Violet's friend was invisible, and he wondered if everyone knew. They probably did.

"He used to live in the house with us. Now he only walks me home from the bus. But when Mom told me about Agatha's baby, he vanished. I was looking for him," Violet admitted as her eyes swept the street again. She sat down on the step, just like her sister waited for her every day.

"You were looking now? Here? Outside?" He looked out and saw nothing. Chris shook his head. Violet's friend had to be invisible.

She sighed. "Yes, but I don't think he wanted Agatha to have a baby."

"But Agatha can't see him?" he asked, sitting down on the step with her.

"Sometimes she does, but it makes her sad. Really sad."

"You can tell when she sees him?"

"Sometimes people don't see me. I'm ultraviolet then," Violet confided.

"I know, you told me on Friday." He chuckled. Chris loved the name she'd given herself and wondered how stealthy she really was.

"I hear things and know things that others don't," Violet whispered.

"Like what?"

"I know about Agatha's baby. Agatha and Mom don't know I know.

But I do," Violet whispered as she looked behind her to make sure nobody else was around.

Chris smiled at the little girl with the big imagination. "Agatha told your mom today about Poppy, remember?"

"Not Poppy, *Jet*. He was born the same day as me, but he died. But he's my friend." Violet looked down at the street as if trying to see her friend.

Leaning back, he looked down at the street to see if he could see Agatha's lost baby waiting for Violet. "I think we have to go inside now. Maybe they're eating already."

"I will introduce you to everyone, but they don't like you," Violet confided.

"Why not?" He already knew that they didn't, but it eluded him what he had done to deserve it.

"Because you will make Agatha sad, just like before." At his stunned expression, she said, "I'm ultraviolet, remember?" She led him into the room full of people who already didn't like him because they thought he had hurt Agatha before and would hurt her again.

Chris was happy that Violet was willing to introduce him to her family because Agatha was busy getting drilled by her sisters about the baby. Not that he was going to remember anyone he had just met since the names and faces were a blur. Even meeting Agatha's sisters was confusing. Nobody looked like Agatha, and none were too happy with him being there.

While two of Agatha's sisters cooked dinner in the kitchen, Chris sat in the living room with Harrison and Jonas. Harrison, he knew, and Jonas he learned was married to Agatha's baby sister, Buzz. They were talking politics, and he was content to just listen to the conversations swirling around him. He did notice that while two of the other men in the family referred to her as Agatha, Buzz and a twin called her Ag. It seemed she was right; only her sisters used the nickname.

"So Agatha has been hiding quite a bit lately. You in particular," Jonas said to him.

"I wouldn't call it hiding; I would call it not sharing right away, letting us have time to get to know each other better." Chris looked around room to see if Agatha was paying attention.

"It was hiding, Chris, Agatha is a clever little secret keeper." Cliff sat forward a little and went on, "So football. My wife says you were good, and my wife is always right."

"Yes, NFL for a year, then blew out my knee," he admitted, though he was surprised he hadn't been thinking about his lost career in a while. His attention had been on other things.

In the kitchen, the twin cooking suddenly looked up and swore, catching everyone's attention. All were looking at her as she dropped the serving spoon on the counter with a loud clatter. "One of the twins needs a diaper change. Maby, help me."

The other twin shook her head. "No diapers. I have told you I do not do diapers."

"Yes, it's a twin thing. Now," the cooking twin demanded and started pushing her sister out of the kitchen and down a hallway until they vanished. Babyless.

"Agatha says you're renovating the house across from her. How is that going?" Jonas asked, as if what just happened hadn't.

"Agatha says not well," Harrison answered for him with a laugh. It seemed Agatha had talked about him, just not in his best light.

Cliff was about to say something but stopped when his wife and her sister came back into the room. His eyes followed her until she gave him a little wave, which he smiled at and leaned back in his chair.

"I wouldn't say not well, just not as expected. I was expecting it to be easier," he admitted as the redhead went into the kitchen.

"Renovations take forever. This house took months longer than we expected, too. But we knew it would take a lot of work when he bought it. It was the perfect house for Sera," Harrison stated and looked around the room. Chris had to admit the house was beautiful.

"What are your plans with the house?" Jonas asked.

"Live in it forever," Harrison answered in confusion.

"I meant Chris. Are you and Agatha going to move over there? Are you going to keep two houses?" Jonas watched as his wife came out of the kitchen.

"Sell it. I never planned to live there." Buzz cast him a look and headed back to her sisters. It was a look that told him he hadn't won her over yet and probably never would.

"The girls are talking," Harrison said of the sisters' odd behavior.

"I know, my wife can't keep a secret. Might be why she wasn't a good reporter." Jonas watched the redhead.

Chris turned to them. "How do you know?"

"They play telephone. One tells another, and so on until they all know. Sometimes the message gets messed up, and sometimes they tell the wrong person. Agatha's baby was quite the surprise." Harrison guessed what that they could be talking about now.

"She was a surprise for Agatha, too. I don't think she ever planned on seeing her again," Chris admitted.

"Agatha can be like that," Jonas said as he watched his wife move across the floor, pretending to tidy up but was just moving from one sister to another, whispering.

Ignoring the comment, Chris asked, "Why don't the sisters look alike?"

Harrison looked at him. "They do. The twins and Harper look a lot alike. Emma and Violet's dad isn't Bradford. Not that it matters to Sera, but it explains a lot."

"I think only Agatha looks different. Buzz fits in better," Jonas said as Lucy, or was it Mabel, announced that the meal was ready. Chris couldn't yet tell them apart when they were separated. Together, it was easy.

Chris waited to get up because there were way too many people heading to the kitchen and saw Agatha do the same thing. When she saw him, she went over, set Poppy on his lap, and sat down.

Sighing, she closed her eyes. "That was as bad as I thought it was going to be."

"But it will pass. In a few days, they won't remember you didn't tell them." He put and arm around her and kissed her head.

"Not in my family. Shit never goes away." She leaned into him further.

"Maybe this time it will." He tried to comfort her.

"Isn't this cute?" one of Agatha's blonde sisters said, looking at them.

"How was fucking Mom's brother at work?" Agatha said and rolled away from Chris so quickly he didn't even know what was happening.

"Shit, Ag, it was never at work!" The blonde dove at Agatha, missing but catching her foot.

Agatha laughed and kicked at her sister, almost shaking her. "Should I tell him about that guy who followed you from France?"

From atop Agatha on the floor, the blonde said, "Should I tell yours about the two that came down from your room buck naked? Where were their clothes, Ag?"

"I don't think they even knew, Harper"

"I know, because you're a shit," Harper said as her husband pulled her off Agatha.

"Really, you two?" Lucy or Mabel said.

"Lucy!" Agatha said from the floor with an evil grin.

"Do not even!" Lucy warned her.

"Agatha! You have a kid now," Sera yelled from the kitchen as Agatha sat up.

"Just reminding them that I know a lot of dirt about them also. Things that they may not want the world to know," Agatha told her mom.

"Okay, everybody back to eating. Agatha, no fighting. Chris, watch her; she's a loose cannon sometimes." Sera scolded her.

"A Grand Cannon?" Buzz asked the crowd. A mixture of laughs and groans responded.

"Buzz, leave Lucy Maud alone." Sera followed the others into the kitchen again.

Agatha lay on the floor, just looking at the ceiling. Chris would've been worried about her if she hadn't been smiling.

"Is Kaine your mom's brother?" Chris asked, reaching out a hand to help her up.

"Yes. They've never been close, though." She ignored the hand and stayed on the floor. "She is still quick. Always was quicker than the twins."

"Maybe you shouldn't fight with her," he suggested.

"I like to remind them they were once kids and to not be so serious."

"You're going to get hurt."

"I always do; they don't hold back. I might have a concussion," she admitted with a grin.

Reaching down, he just grabbed her hand and pulled her to her feet. Instantly, he checked her eyes to see if she did have a concussion. She hadn't been hit hard, he checked anyway. As he did that, she rubbed her head. Once he was sure she was fine, they went into the kitchen. Seeing this new version of Agatha was unusual. It was a side he hadn't really seen over the last weeks.

During the meal, nobody said anything about what happened in the living room. Conversation circled around the babies already born and those yet to come.

Chris couldn't get over how different the meal was from the somber meals at his mother's house, a place where the china and crystal was always used. His siblings mostly just ate and didn't say much. After eating with the Lovelys, he didn't know how he was going to go back to that type of dining experience. Not after this one.

As the meal came to a close, Agatha decided that Poppy should go home, declaring that the day was too much for the baby, who, for her part, started rubbing her eyes, as if her mom told her to do it.

After saying goodbye and heading down the street, he was relieved that it was over. Now he had met her family and learned a lot about Agatha. Nothing about her surprised him anymore. She was unique and more different than he had ever suspected when they met, but everything made him like her even more.

CHAPTER TWENTY-EIGHT

THE NEXT WEEK was odd for Agatha. First, Violet did not come over after school; she just went home because her mom was home with baby Benji. Second, living with Poppy was a completely new experience. Someone was dependent on her at all times. No longer could she spend all night drawing if she wanted to. Agatha had to be able to get up in the morning when her baby wanted to eat.

Turning around her internal clock had been a challenge, though Chris helped by already being on the same internal clock as Poppy, reminding Agatha to go to bed at night and sometimes carrying her there. Then he'd wake her up as the sun came up. She had eventually stopped needing the timers she had set for herself. She had Chris, after all.

Chris started to come home at lunchtime and stay there, taking care of Poppy so she could work on her book. He didn't know it was a book, but he let her draw just the same. She wanted to tell him, but then she would have to tell him everything.

When he knew everything, he would leave. And in her heart, she knew that she might be good enough to fuck, but not to date. That's who she would always be. And once he realized it, as much as it hurt her, he would be gone.

She knew she would and did love him for all his faults and flaws, but he didn't love her. This, whatever it was, was just a distraction for him. Until he figured out what he wanted to do with his life. She had no place in the future life he would live.

After spending most of the afternoon writing the words for her book, she slipped all the pages into a large file folder. It was done. She would review it a few more times, but it was exactly how she wanted it.

Humming a song she had last been listening to, she headed downstairs to see her baby and her baby's dad. Agatha caught sight of them on the couch snuggled together, Chris reading Poppy a book. The baby was looking at it intently. In his baritone, Chris read the familiar words to her daughter.

Walking right to him, Agatha pulled the book from his hands and looked at it. "What the fuck? Where did you get this?"

Since he had found her that day in her studio, he hadn't spent any time up there. Or so she thought. He'd let her have her space and to work alone. How had he found a book she kept in the far corner of that room? What else had he found?

Confusion crossed his face and he said, "I bought it the day I bought the crib."

"Why?" She tossed the book across the room, as far from him as possible. It had a moose on the cover and was one that she had worked on as Poppy grew inside her. Drawing had been her distraction then, a distraction from thinking about him.

"What?" He shook his head as he watched the book land on the floor.

"Why did you buy it?" Agatha took her daughter away from him.

"It's a book, Agatha. Can't I read to her?" He crossed his now empty arms.

"Why did you buy it?" she asked again as her voice clogged with unshed tears. The time had finally come. Whatever this was, was over. He was going to be gone soon. Today.

"I do not have to explain myself to you," he hissed.

Was he lying about buying the book? Had he found it up in her studio after all? Had he seen everything in her private corner, a place nobody belonged? A place she kept her deepest secrets. Did he know them all?

"Get out." Fighting back the tears, she turned and walked toward the kitchen. It was snack time after all, and her daughter was hungry.

He got up from the chair and followed her. "Excuse me? You're kicking me out because I *read* to her? News flash, Agatha, you're supposed to read to your kids!"

"It's not the damn book, it's you. It's me. Just get out now." Agatha steeled herself against the pain as she turned to him, wishing he would just leave and get it over with.

"No, I am not leaving. I love you, Agatha. I want to spend my life with you." He said the words she had longed to hear since she was seven years old. Except they weren't true. He didn't even know her.

Clenching her daughter to her, she glared at him. "Until when, Chris? Until your friends show up? Will I be good enough then? When your family knows about us? Why don't you just leave now before anyone finds out about us. Save yourself the embarrassment of people thinking we're a couple."

Glaring down at her, his nose flared as he asked, "What are you even talking about?"

"You remember everyone, Chris! Everyone but me. Am I so forgettable? For ten years, your locker was beside mine. Ten years. Nine years later, you don't even remember me!" she yelled as the baby started to cry. She knew she shouldn't be yelling with Poppy in her arms, but she couldn't control it anymore. "Remember, Chris? I'm good enough to fuck, but you would never date me. Seems to me that's exactly what's happening now."

There, she'd said it, but there was no relief at getting it off her chest. All she felt was hollow, gutted by what she knew he was thinking now. That being here was a mistake. Just like always.

He ran his hands through his curly hair in frustration. "What?" Did he finally remember her? Or was she still a nobody? Both options tore at Agatha's heart because she didn't know which was worse.

"You always forget me. I'm Agatha Christie Lovely, every day. For fucking ever. Now get out of my house. I will not let you read my books to my kid. Ever." Brokenhearted and furious, Agatha turned and ran out the back door with Poppy still in her arms. Whether he followed or not, she didn't know. Since he didn't catch her, she knew he hadn't. There was no way she could outrun him, especially with Poppy in her arms.

Agatha was shaking so bad by the time she got to Sera's house that she could barely open the door to the back porch. She couldn't even make it into to the kitchen. Knocking didn't gain her entrance either. Sitting in the corner of her mom's back porch, Agatha cried as she tried to soothe the sobbing baby. She tried to tell her baby that it would be okay, that they would be okay. They didn't need Daddy. They didn't need anyone.

CHAPTER TWENTY-NINE

Standing in the middle of Agatha Christie Lovely's kitchen, Chris couldn't think. How had he never seen it? Of course, the last time he had seen her, he had been hungover, but he had recognized her that night.

When she had been stick-thin with wild hair, he recognized her because that was how she had looked and acted when they were in high school. But it had never been the real her. The real her was the woman in this house with the wicked sense of humor and quick wit. She was the amazing woman he wanted to spend his life with, but underneath it all was her prickly side, the side that she hid her real self behind. She had been hurt by him, time and time again. Hurt by the immature guy who thought that because he could run with a football, he was better than anyone else.

She had been the first face he had seen when he had arrived at PS12 for the first time. She was carrying a plastic bag full of supplies that all the kids needed for the school year—just her and her bag, no mom or dad. When he saw her, he wished his own parents weren't there; they were just fighting anyway. In class they had been assigned to sit together because their names, Lowell and Lovely, were close in the alphabet. She had long black hair and a red headband to hold it off her face. By the next week, she had been moved to a different table because she could already read. They never sat at the same table again that year because she was smart, and he was not.

The next year, they were not in the same class at all. He only saw her on the playground. That year, all the kids liked to play a game called kiss or kill. It was like tag, but if you caught the person, you could choose to kiss them or kill them, aka knock them to the ground. That year he kissed her once and killed her fifteen times. Because she was a girl. By Christmas, she was no longer in his recess group, which had confused him, and he wondered what happened to her. He had never found out.

In second grade, she wasn't in his class or his recess, but he saw her in the hallway every now and again.

When third grade rolled around, she was in his class again. When they were assigned seats together, he would watch her draw on any paper she could find. She drew almost anything, and you could always tell what it was. One day he told her that she was good at drawing, and she told him he was not. But they still sat at the same table, and sometimes she'd give him her drawings when she was done. That was also the year she had changed her name from Chrissy to Christie. He talked to her almost every day, and he had considered her his best friend that year.

Fourth grade had been a bad year for their friendship. One day, he had been mad at his dad and had slammed open his locker and hit Christie in the face. Her head was bleeding, but she didn't cry at first. She just looked at him in disbelief, then she cried. The teacher had taken her to the office, and she had been gone the rest of the day. When she had come back to school, she had worn a Band-Aid on her head for a week. After the Band-Aid had come off, he could still see the cut. He had scarred her. He had given her a card and tried to say hi to her every day, but that didn't alleviate his guilt about hurting her.

Sucking in a breath, Chris realized that the scar on her forehead wasn't from her sister; it was from him. He had scarred her for life.

In fifth grade, he said hi to her every day, and some days, she returned the greeting. He had almost asked her to a dance that year but had chickened out. She would never say yes to someone like him. Their lockers had been together again, and he accidentally hit her in the head with his locker fifteen times, but she was kind of short, and never once did he make her bleed.

Sixth grade meant a new school, and he called her Christie like everyone else, no special nickname anymore. He started football and loved it. Again, he almost asked her to a dance, but he overheard her telling her friend she never went to dances, so he didn't. She was one of the few to give out valentines, his said Christopher, which was not on the list, so she had made it special for him. He accidentally hit her in the head with his locker twelve times that year because she was very small still.

In seventh grade, he couldn't remember hitting her with his locker door at all, which was a bonus, but they shared none of the same classes that year. When she came back from summer vacation, she had short hair. It was cute but different. That was the year girls started to notice him, but not Christie. He received his last valentine from her that year, though he didn't hand out any. It had a bunny she had drawn on it. He had kept it for years.

When eighth grade came, he had girls chasing him, so he dated a few of them over the year. He still said hi to her whenever she said hi to him. It was the same until junior year, when they shared an empty locker, using it to store their coats. He smelled her perfume every time he put his coat on. Sometimes he worried that the guys would notice, but mostly he liked smelling her when he wore the jacket.

Senior year, that's when he really got to know Christie Lovely. In science class, she was snarky and admitted that science wasn't her thing. That year she finally started going to parties and never cared what others thought of her. She was who she was, and if you don't like her, too bad. She was far braver than he was.

When he and his girlfriend broke up, he almost asked her out in science class but didn't. He wasn't her type. Not that he saw her dating anyone, but a brilliant artist wouldn't have any interest in a jock.

Then came the party right before graduation. She had asked him to dance. He decided to say "screw you" to his friends and all their snide remarks and danced with her. He had always wanted to dance with her. In his arms, she was as small as he had always thought she would be, small and perfect. She had rested her head on his shoulder, and it was like they were alone. He had even gotten up the nerve to kiss her. When the song ended, his friends dragged him away laughing.

Later he had hid out from the guys in a bedroom upstairs because they wouldn't leave him alone about dancing with Christie. They all thought that he had done it as a joke on her because they couldn't see how he would be interested in her. After a while, he decided it was time to leave the party, but the moment he stepped out the door, he found her in the hallway, looking as lost and alone as he felt. Pulling her into that room had been as natural as dancing with her. Then he had kissed her and more, way more. Sex with Christie had been different then with girlfriend, Savannah, but it took years for him to realize why. It took until he found Agatha to know why. With Agatha, it wasn't about him feeling good; it was about making *her* feel good. His orgasm took second place to hers for the first time in his life.

After that night, all he could think about was dating Christie. He had even planned their first date. He'd take her for pizza and a walk along the river maybe that next Monday night. Without having her phone number, he had no way to contact her until school on Monday.

But on Monday, he had been confronted by his friends the moment he had gotten to school, and he had messed up. When they demanded to know what had happened, he had played off their night together as nothing but sex. But that had just been for the guys; they didn't need to know how special she was.

When Jason had laughed and said Christie was behind him, his heart sank. He knew he had never messed up so much. Turning to see her face, Chris knew his words had hurt her as she was pale and nearly in tears. His eyes went to the scar still on her forehead, and his heart twisted at how his words and actions have caused her pain.

Before he could say anything, she turned and left the school. She never came back, skipping the last week and graduation, where they would have sat side-by-side as they had since kindergarten. Without her, the day had been gloomy and lifeless. Or maybe that was because of the whiskey he had been drinking since that morning.

He hadn't seen her again until that party when he knew it was her. He had watched her serving food for an hour before he realized who she was. But he had waited until he was too drunk to do anything but fuck her. He didn't even know if he said he was sorry that night.

Now he had blown it once again by not recognizing her. They had spent over a month together, yet he'd ignored every little clue. She had never asked him about himself; she had already known. That first day, she had been prickly and distant because she remembered him and everything he had done to her.

Chris wondered why she had changed her name. She must have always gone by her middle name in school. Picking up the moose book, he wondered why she had chosen to use the name she'd used in school for her books.

Since he had moved in across the street from her, he had been drawn to her like he never had with anyone else. Something in him knew her and knew he could love her. Knew he *would* love her, but now she was gone. This time she hadn't kicked him out of her house; she had left him in it. This was her safe place, and he had hurt her so bad that she had left.

He had no idea how to convince her he had changed because it seemed he hadn't. Every time they were together, he had hurt her a little more. And this time, what he had done was unforgivable.

CHAPTER THIRTY

AFTER HARRISON HAD FOUND her on his back porch with nothing but her daughter and in tears, the sisters had been shifting Agatha and Poppy from one house to the next. Not that Chris was ever getting close to finding her, but because each sister got tired of her pretty quickly.

Within hours of her fight with Chris, she and Poppy were at Harper's place since Kaine and Harper had the room for two extra people. But since Poppy had suddenly been uprooted from her home again, she was not happy and cried all night long. There had been nothing Agatha could do. She had been a mom for a week and was struggling with her own heartbreak.

So the next day, she had been shifted to Lucy and Leo's house, but with their six kids, she was ready to leave within the hour. There were too many people, even if they weren't even all home at the same time.

By nightfall, she had moved to Mabel and Cliff's. They had stayed for two days. Poppy loved Cliff, which was no surprise; the man had a way with women. Mabel let Agatha do her thing, sometimes. It seemed since marriage and making a home with her new husband, Mabel had become more particular about everything having a place. And babies made more of a mess than she had been expecting. Not to mention that after months of being married, Mabel and Cliff were still very much in the honeymoon stage. Their constant affection made her remember the few short days she and Chris were happy, and it made her heart hurt worse.

Today they had moved on to Buzz and Jonas's place. It was her last refuge that wasn't on the same street as Chris. Her emotions were frayed.

Buzz was in her last week of pregnancy and was not excited about having house guests and did nothing to make them comfortable. Jonas tried, but his wife was a snarler, so he couldn't do much either.

Buzz was laid out on the couch, watching a show on buying wedding dresses, which caused her to either cry hysterically or yell curse words at the screen—there was no middle ground. Agatha was playing with a box of toys Jonas had found in the baby's room for Poppy to play with.

"How the fuck did you do this without anyone knowing?" Buzz demanded. Whether she was talking to the TV or her, Agatha didn't know.

Deciding to just let her sister yell, she handed a blue block to her dark-haired baby. After the first night of crying, Poppy had settled down and was accepting the changes in her life way better than her mom was. Agatha hated everything that was happening and wanted to go home, but she had to stay away from there until it was completely Chris-free again. However long that took.

Not just home, but to a time when Chris liked her and loved their baby. Those days felt like her most happy memories. Not that their time together had been real, but it had felt like it, to her at least.

"Earth to Agatha! Answer me!" Buzz was looking at her.

"*What?*" she barked back.

"How did you have a baby without us knowing?" Buzz repeated the question.

"I didn't think it was so hard. Maybe I had an easier pregnancy," Agatha answered, not mentioning that her sister might be overdoing the complaining a little.

Buzz flopped her head back on the couch. "Did it hurt?"

"Did what hurt?"

"Pushing a human out of your vagina!" Buzz yelled at the ceiling.

"Yes." Agatha didn't elaborate.

"Is that all you're going to say about it?" Buzz demanded as she shifted to glare at her.

Agatha finally snapped. "Yes, because you're already yelling at me. Do I need to tell you it feels like your insides are coming out? Or that your body feels like it's going to rip apart, and that it kind of does? Is that what you want to know? That the baby is a slimy, wiggling thing that they toss at you only to turn back to your vagina?!" Buzz was turning a little paler with Agatha's words.

"Not really what I wanted to hear, but I guess I deserved it," Buzz admitted. "Maybe I just wanted to hear the 'it's worth it' speech."

"It is." Agatha sighed and hugged Poppy to her.

"How did you give her up? I'm already so in love with Jonas's spawn. I couldn't." Buzz sat up as she rubbed her stomach.

"I thought that she would be better off without me. I had been fired and hadn't been able to find a new job for weeks. Even the Grog wouldn't hire me anymore. I had submitted a book to a publisher but hadn't heard back, which meant they didn't like it. I had nothing and was going nowhere. I couldn't take a kid down with me. I knew that."

"Mom would have raised her in a heartbeat," Buzz stated the obvious.

"I know she would have, but one day, she would have told Poppy that I was her mom. And then she would know that her mom was a loser who couldn't make something of life. Then she would think that that failing was in her too, that she's a loser like me."

"Is that what you think, Agatha? That you are a loser?"

"I have always been the artsy weirdo, Buzz. Always."

"Agatha Christie Lovely, you are the most talented person I have ever met. We have all been just waiting for you to find your calling. It could have been anything! Everything you draw, paint, and even sketch is amazing. Art isn't easy; we all know that. We let you do what you wanted because you had to find your way."

"I had no ambition," Agatha said as Poppy crawled away from her.

"Maybe not for bartending and waitressing, but every day you created art in your room. You never stopped, because that's what you wanted to do. We were all shiftless for a while. Only Sera ever really had a plan for her life. Harper and Lucy struggled to start their catering business. Maby has never struggled, but she's Maby. Me, I still don't know what I want to be when I grow up, but I married well, so I don't have to." Buzz laughed at herself.

Agatha pointed to her stomach. "You're going to be a mom."

"I am, but you already are, and you're killing it. I hope I'm half as good as you are at it." Buzz leaned back on the couch. "I worry about that."

"You are going to be so much better than me. I didn't even know if I want to be a mom or could be a good one. Or if I'm just messing her up."

"You practically raised Violet so that Mom could work," Buzz pointed out.

"But Violet was her baby, not mine. Sera always came home at the end of the day."

"But she didn't need to. In fact, she sometimes didn't. She had you. Maybe I should keep you, and you can raise this one." She tapped her belly.

"You can't afford me." Agatha laughed

"I have access to a sexy, rich man's checkbook. I can afford anything." Buzz grinned, most likely thinking about her sexy man since his checkbook had never mattered to her. No matter how often she complained, she never updated anything. In fact, she had on a sweatshirt that had belonged to Mabel during her college days.

"I have to focus of raising Poppy right now." Agatha watched the baby pull herself up to stand by the couch.

"Did you tell the dad about her?"

"I don't know who the daddy is," Agatha lied.

Buzz's laugh scared Poppy, and she fell onto her butt, crying. Buzz stopped laughing and pulled the baby up to sit with her. "Your mommy is such a kidder. She thinks Aunty Buzz is stupid. Aunty Buzz was there too."

"You were not; I was covering for you," Agatha stated, then slammed her hand over her mouth.

"Suddenly, you remember." Buzz grinned at her. "And you can thank me with cash or babysitting. I might want babysitting more than cash."

"I am not talking about it."

"You don't have to. I have an imagination. Just one question, though. Was it in a public location?" Buzz asked, playing pattycake with Poppy.

"It was not!" she hissed at her sister, then remembered it wasn't that far from a public location.

"Is Mommy blushing, Poppy?" Buzz asked. "Must be a pretty hot memory."

"Let your imagination go wild, Buzz. It's the best you'll get."

"Oh, don't worry, I am. But on a more serious note, Ag, this kid is adorable. I mean from you and him to this? Crazy. Maybe you carry more of my genes than I ever thought."

"Thank you, Buzz. I think she's pretty cute myself," Agatha said and left her sister with the baby. It had been a long few days, and she hadn't had much time without her daughter. Buzz could watch Poppy so that Agatha could take a nap or dwell on her lonely future. Whichever happened.

Alone in her room, she crawled into bed fully clothed and curled into a ball. Buzz was right; everyone in the family supported her in any way possible. So they never said the words out loud, but they believed in her. From finding her jobs that wouldn't interfere with her drawing time to making sure she had food when they knew she wouldn't put forth effort or time to make it. They never teased her about something that could have just been a hobby. It was with that silent support that she had been able to finish not one but six of her books before they even all moved out of the house.

If she had been brave enough to tell them about Poppy when she was pregnant, they would have given her the same support. Not one would have told her that she couldn't or shouldn't raise her daughter. They would have been there for every appointment and late-night feeding she allowed them to be at. In fact, seeing them rally around Buzz and Lucy when they each were pregnant and alone, she knew they would have done the same for her.

Now she had to learn how to lean on them more than she had in the past. They want her to lean on them. They always had.

CHAPTER THIRTY-ONE

AGATHA HAD BEEN GONE for days, and Chris knew it was stupid to sit on his step waiting for her to come out at 3 p.m., but he did it anyway. Violet's mom was on maternity leave, so she wasn't coming down here anyway. But just like he had every day this week, he sat and waited.

There was nothing else he could do. She didn't answer her phone. Sera wouldn't give her his messages; in fact, she wouldn't even talk to him. He had no idea where any of her sisters lived. His only connection to her was her house, which she had abandoned.

By 3:30 p.m., he knew she wasn't coming out, but he still hadn't given up the hope that she would. Just then, a SUV stopped in front of the house. A blonde woman jumped out of the driver's seat and hurried to the front door, quickly unlocked it, and went inside.

The blonde was not Agatha's mom; it was her sister. Maybe she would talk to him. With speed he hadn't needed for over a year, he rushed to the house. The door wasn't locked, so he went inside. It looked exactly same as the last time he had been inside, only it felt different, empty.

"Hello, anyone home?" He knew she was there, but he didn't need her calling the cops on him.

"Fuck! You gave me a heart attack," Harper said from the doorway of the kitchen, a hand pressed to her chest.

"Sorry to scare you. I'm trying to find Agatha."

"She's not here." She huffed and turned and went back into the kitchen.

"But you know where she is." It was not a question.

"Yes, I do, but you don't need to know that information." Chris followed to find her digging in the pantry.

"Please, Harper. I just need to talk to her again. Just for a minute, please," Chris pleaded. At this point, he wasn't beyond begging, but he knew better than to get too close to the woman.

"So you remember me then? Must just be my sister you can't remember," Harper stated, slamming a pile of paper plates onto the counter.

"I'm sorry I didn't recognize her. She's changed over the last few years," Chris said, not wanting to go into it with this woman. All he wanted to do was explain it to Agatha.

"Some of us like those changes." She tossed some plastic cups on the island that her mom and sisters sat at on Saturday mornings, just not this last Saturday. Nobody had been here on Saturday morning. He had been watching.

"I don't know what to say to you, Harper." He ran his fingers through his hair. He didn't know how to get the woman he loved back. Frustration and defeat were all he felt, and he knew that neither were going to get her to come back to him.

"I don't know either, Chris. Agatha is special; she always has been. She doesn't let many into her world. She may put out this image of being emotionless, but she isn't. Her hurts run deep." Harper slammed a container of plastic forks on the counter next.

"When did she start going by Agatha?" he asked. It was a small detail, but he wanted to know everything about her.

"Birth!"

"She went by Christie in school," he reminded her.

"Because some little shithead in kindergarten made fun of her name. She couldn't pronounce it right, and he made fun of her a lot."

She stopped digging in the cabinet as she spoke, her anger visible. "After that, she went by Christie in school, but at home, she was always Agatha."

"The men in your family don't call her Ag. Why?" If she was willing to talk to him, he wanted to get more answers.

"Because she doesn't let them. Buzz is the same way. She is Bea to the world, but at home, she goes by Buzz. You have to be special to call her Buzz," Harper said, going back to digging in the cabinet.

"I want to see her," he pushed, trying again.

"That's not up to me. She has to come back when she's ready." Harper gathered up all the paper products and headed for the door. He could tell she was done talking to him, and he wasn't going to get anything from her. Not today.

"Can you just tell her that I want to see her?" he asked, following her through the living room, still strewn with Poppy's things. Agatha hadn't taken much when she had walked out and hadn't been back for any of it. The book she had thrown was still on the floor, just where it had landed.

"I can, but she's hiding," Harper said, letting him open the front door for her.

"From me?" He knew he shouldn't ask, because he already knew the answer.

"From everyone," Harper stated, not looking at him. Her answer told him that her family might know where she was, but she was hiding from them also. Hiding right in front of them.

After locking the door, he helped Harper into her SUV. As he watched her drive away, he wondered if she would tell her sister he wanted to talk to her. At this point, he had no clue.

All he knew was that he wasn't going to find Agatha. She would stay away as long as he was around, leaving him no way to see her or speak to her. She wouldn't let him explain anything to her. He wanted to tell her he had changed from that dumb kid she had known before. He had realized now what was important in life. It was her. It had always been her.

CHAPTER THIRTY-TWO

THE HOUSE WAS COMING TOGETHER QUICKLY with the contractor and his team doing all the work and Chris staying out of the way. They had the kitchen nearly finished, and the hardwoods had been laid on the entire second floor. But Chris's heart wasn't in the remodel anymore; his entire focus was on the empty house across the street, waiting to see if a certain sister showed up. If anyone showed up.

His talk with Harper the day before had cleared up some, but not all, of the questions he had about Agatha. He wondered if he was the boy who had made fun of her name, but he couldn't remember. *It did sound like something I would've done,* he thought in shame.

In an attempt to find out, he had decided to visit his mom, who couldn't remember anything about his elementary school years and didn't want to. But he grabbed a box that contained his yearbooks and some other mementos and took them to his house.

As he looked through the box, he glanced out the window at Agatha's dark house. She must be missing her studio. It had been days since she had been there. He wondered if Poppy could walk yet. He was missing her more than he expected to, but he figured that she was a small part of the woman he loved, so naturally, he loved her as well.

In the box he found his kindergarten yearbook, their pictures side by side. Agatha had a toothy grin that was already a little sassy, yet Chris was missing most of his teeth and had barely smiled for the picture. Even now, he could remember how he had thought she was cute back then. It also made him realize how much Poppy looked like her mom.

As he paged through other yearbooks, he watched her change and grow up, himself always alongside her. In the fourth grade, she had cut her hair into a short style much like her current one. He noticed that she'd grown it out again so that she had long hair in her senior picture. He remembered that by the end of the year, it was short again.

He recalled that she had said her dad left when she was in junior high, but he saw no evidence that his leaving had affected her, other than the fact that her clothes went from brightly colored T-shirts to black. Or maybe that was how it affected her; his leaving took her love of color with him.

Putting the yearbooks aside, he took out articles and clippings from his football career. Those held no interest for him at all once he caught sight of something he thought had been tossed out years before: a valentine with a hand-drawn bunny on it with the words "Somebunny Loves You" written in cursive and Christie's name at the bottom. He wondered now if she had drawn it especially for him or if she had just given him one she had drawn, not carrying what it said.

After repacking the box, he set it in the corner, leaving the card out. Whichever of Agatha's sisters he saw next, he would send the card with her to give to Agatha. Maybe then Agatha would talk to him.

With no other idea what to do, Chris returned to sitting on his front step, knowing she wasn't coming out today. She was still hiding.

But he sat and stared anyway; there was nothing else to do. His contractor no longer let him help. It seemed that even under supervision, he couldn't get anything done right. This included him having to have a toilet replaced three times.

As cars passed and kids yelled from somewhere, Chris looked at the house he wanted to be in with Agatha and Poppy as a family.

"Boy, are you depressing to look at," someone said from the sidewalk.

Looking over at a brown-haired guy in a suit and blue tie, he sat up. He had no idea who the guy was, but he was happy someone wanted to talk to him. Without Agatha and Poppy around, he was bored.

"Thanks, just letting my mind wander."

"Toward some Lovely lady, I assume. They dig their claws into you, and you can't shake them. Even when they disappear." The man sat down near him and looked at the house as well.

"What are you talking about?" Chris asked in confusion. The man was talking in riddles.

"You missing Agatha," the man stated.

"Do you know her?" Chris turned to the guy, excited. Maybe he could tell him where to find Agatha.

"You have no memory at all!" The man laughed. "Or maybe you weren't paying attention to anyone but Agatha that night. I'm married to the lovely Maby Lovely. My name's Cliff."

"Chris Lowell." Chris shook the man's hand, but still didn't remember him from the dinner at Agatha's mom's house. Cliff was right; his eyes had been on Agatha that night, and her daughter.

"That I know. I should beat you up for sleeping in my woman's bed, but I can account for her movements that night, so I'm okay." Cliff chuckled.

Chris shrugged. "Thanks for letting me off so easy."

"Any time. But do not, I repeat, do not touch my woman," Cliff warned, not that Chris was a threat on that front. If she hadn't looked exactly like her twin sister, Chris wouldn't even remember her, but identical twins tended to be memorable.

Chris raised his hands in the air. "I will leave her be."

"Good, now show me your house. What are you doing with it?" Cliff got to his feet.

"Selling it once it's done. I really like how it is turning out," Chris admitted, though he was not really responsible for its appearance.

After showing Cliff around the house and telling him everything that had been done and everything that was going to be done, Chris was surprised with how many questions Cliff had. But it made the morning go quickly.

"So when are you going to be done?" Cliff asked as they made their way back outside.

"Two weeks, I think. Two weeks," he repeated, looking back at Agatha's house.

Cliff patted him on the shoulder. "She won't come back until you're gone, no matter how long it takes."

"I know. I just miss her," he admitted to this virtual stranger.

"It's the claws; they dig in deep. But it doesn't hurt as bad when they're around," Cliff said.

Both their eyes followed a white Jeep that pulled to a stop in front of Agatha's house. Both watched with interest as a brunette climbed from the driver's seat and waved at them.

"Your wife?" Chris asked, because it was either her or her twin.

"Nope, that's Lucy," he replied, walking toward the woman.

Cliff gave Lucy a hug when they reached her. "Did you bring the babies or kids?"

"Nope, Leo's home with the boys, and the girls are all with their mothers," Lucy explained as she opened the back end of the Jeep.

"And you?" Cliff asked.

"I'm making desserts for tomorrow night. My kitchen—for now—only has one oven. This one has two. Harper is coming to help." She started handing the men things to carry into the house.

"Just like old times," Cliff said as his arms were filled with baking supplies.

"Except no one's here." Lucy rushed to open the door for them, her arms empty.

"I know, it's creepy. It's never this empty. I remember one morning waking up in your room, and everyone had someone over. Well, not my Maby, but everyone else did. It was a fucking madhouse." Cliff set his load on the counter, and Chris followed suit.

"I know, and now it's empty. Agatha and the baby will be back one day," she said, looking right at Chris with a glare. "What are you doing in the neighborhood, Clifton?"

"I am going to buy my lady love a house." Cliff grinned at her.

"You've already bought her a house," Lucy pointed out, ignoring Chris.

"She doesn't really like it, so I'm going to buy Chris's. She'll love living next to Agatha and having Mom Lovely right down the street. And I know she loves older houses rather than new ones."

Chris stared at Cliff. He had said nothing about wanting to buy the house, just that he wanted to see it. His heart sank. He had a buyer, but he still wanted to live there so that he knew when Agatha came home.

"You didn't say anything about buying it," Chris stated.

"Soon, I will buy it. You should get one on this street too," Cliff said to Lucy.

"No way, this house is tiny compared to Leo's. With six kids, we need all the room we can get. Maybe when the two big ones are gone, but maybe not then either. I kind of like where we're at," Lucy said.

"Your loss, Luce," Cliff said. "I have to get to work before my lady love realizes I'm not there."

With a hug to his sister-in-law, he was off, leaving the room in a vacuum of silence between Chris and Lucy.

"Have you seen Agatha?"

"Not today."

"You have the twins?" he asked, even though he knew she did. There were two car seats in the back of her vehicle. He just wanted to make conversation.

"Yes, that's me." She didn't elaborate.

"I love Agatha. Everything about her." He decided to lay it out there for her sister.

For days he has just wanted to talk to Agatha, but if he had to go through her sister, he would. If pouring his heart out to this woman would get his Agatha to come back, he would do it.

"Did you tell her?" Lucy asked, her attention fully on him now.

"Yes, but it was too late. She was already mad at me for reading to Poppy."

"Her books, Chris. Her own family had only known she had published them for just a few weeks. She doesn't share easily."

He sat down on a stool. "I know. She hid that she was an artist from me until after we had slept together."

"You and your friends made fun of her for being an artist. I don't even think anyone at the school knew she had gotten into art school." Lucy started pulling out ingredients.

"She must have loved art school." He could see her there, talking colors with her like-minded friends.

"She quit after three weeks. No explanation. Then Mom had Violet, and Agatha was her nanny until Violet went to school. Agatha bartended at night usually." Lucy shifted her ingredients around.

"What are we talking about?" Harper interrupted as she came into the room, carrying more food.

"Just telling Chris about Agatha and art school," Lucy told her sister.

"I don't remember her going to art school," Harper said.

"You were in France. It only lasted a few weeks. Then she was home," Lucy said.

"See? I missed too much being over there," Harper complained.

"Did Agatha say why she didn't go to graduation?" he asked innocently.

"Nope, but that does sound like Agatha to quit school with only a week to go. They had to mail her a diploma," Lucy said with a laugh.

"You're right," said Harper. "I didn't come home for her graduation. I came home when Violet was born." She laughed at her sister's antics.

"Did Agatha miscarry the day Violet was born?" Violet's story had bothered him for weeks now, and he had to ask.

"What?" Lucy turned to him in shock.

"No!" Harper stated. "Who told you that?"

"Violet said something about it. It seemed so real the way she talked about the baby," Chris stated. Her conviction was what had made him feel it was true.

"Violet is nine and has no idea what a miscarriage is. Also, if it happened the day she was born, she would have no clue," Lucy stated.

"That's what I was hoping. I didn't want Agatha to have gone through that," he answered with relief. Lucy was right; Violet would have no idea, and there was no way Agatha was pregnant nine years ago. He knew her nine years ago.

"What did Violet say?" Harper grabbed a towel and wiped her hands as she rounded the island and sat on a stool farthest from his.

"Nothing really. Just that her invisible friend is Agatha's baby and that she was mad her mom told her about Poppy in front of him because he disappeared."

"I think she made it all up," Harper stated. "Kids tell stories."

"I hope so," Chris said.

The room fell silent, and Harper got back up to help her sister. Within minutes they were discussing the event they were planning the next day, forgetting that he was even there. He let them and just listened for any word of Agatha, but there were none.

Not wanting to be in the way, he said goodbye and reminded them that he wanted to talk to Agatha. Both said they would say something to her, but he didn't know them well enough to know if they would or not.

It was two hours later that he remembered the valentine. Running upstairs, he grabbed it and took it across the street. Both sisters were sitting in the living room watching TV, not cooking at all anymore. But the house smelled like chocolate and lemon. It was heavenly.

"Can one of you do me a favor?" he asked. He hadn't knocked, and they hadn't cared.

"What?" Lucy tipped her head back and looked up at him like an annoyed sister would.

"Can you give Agatha this? But tell her that I want it back one day. No burning it, no throwing it, no ripping it up," he said.

Lucy sat up and looked at him.

"We're mean people, but not that mean. What is it?" Harper asked.

Handing the card to them, he watched them both look at it and then at him. "You kept this?"

"Yes, she made it. It's special. Nobody had given me a handmade valentine before."

"We'll get it back to you," Lucy swore and wiped a tear from her eye.

"Thank you. I know she thinks I don't remember her, but I do. I remember so much. I just want to tell her," he said and walked away. All he could do was hope that they passed the message on to their sister.

He was quickly running out of options on getting her back. If her sisters wouldn't help, he knew he had no chance with her. Once his house was complete, he would have no reason to stay and wait for her. Time would be up.

CHAPTER THIRTY-THREE

Poppy was finally asleep. Sure, the borrowed bed had blue sheets and blankets, but she didn't care—a nursery was a nursery. Running a hand over the baby-soft curls on Poppy's head, she missed the man who gave her the curls.

Yesterday, Harper had told her that Chris wanted to talk to her, but she didn't push her to call him. She just had a message. She also asked if Chris made fun of her in kindergarten, but Agatha couldn't remember anything that far back.

Leaving her baby in the nursery, she went to her assigned bedroom, far away from the master. It was up to Buzz and Jonas to get Poppy if she woke up in the night. They needed the practice, and she didn't want to be close enough to hear anything.

Sitting back in her bed, she grabbed the sketchpad she had brought. Though she couldn't draw her books in it, she could sketch how she wanted her next book to go. Creating ideas for her next story wasn't as easy as one would think, especially after she'd just finished one.

As she erased a skunk, her bedroom door burst open. Expecting to see Buzz, she was surprised when Harper and Lucy walked into the room, Buzz following behind.

"We have to talk, Agatha," Harper stated angrily.

"What did I do?" she asked. She had done a lot in the last few weeks, and more over the last few years. Pinning down what she had done wrong in their eyes this time was going to be hard.

"First, Chris gave us this today to give to you. A peace offering." Lucy handed her the piece of paper she had been holding carefully.

Looking at the paper, Agatha was confused for a half a second, and then realized it was the valentine she had given him years before. Somebunny did love him. She had. At the time, she was sure he had thrown it away. She watched him throw all his valentines away that afternoon, but he had kept hers.

"Thanks," she mumbled as she stared at it in disbelief.

"Are you still that somebunny, Agatha?" Harper sat on the bed.

"It doesn't matter. I'm not what he wants; never have been. And now he knows who I am." She put the card in her sketchpad and closed it.

"He seems to still like you, Agatha. He said he loved you today." Lucy crawled under the covers next to her, leaned against the headboard, and put an arm around Agatha.

"Once his friends find out, he'll forget about what he said," Agatha told them.

"Not this time. He isn't a kid anymore, Agatha," Harper stated, sitting down but still a bit angry with her.

"I can't do it again," Agatha replied, fighting back tears. She didn't want to cry in front of her sisters.

"Maybe you won't have to. Maybe he won't break your heart this time." Lucy squeezed her.

"He already did," Agatha whispered.

"I don't know. I think you ran off on him. I think his heart is broken too," Harper stated.

"He'll get on with his life; he always does," Agatha told her. This had happened before.

"Not this time. Cliff wants to buy Chris's house, and his only reaction was sadness. That house is his only connection to you." Harper squeezed her foot.

"At least he'll be gone soon." Agatha's heart hurt saying the words.

"Why did you quit high school, Agatha?" Harper folded her arms.

"Because I was done. I just stayed home that day; it was the last week anyway. I wasn't good at it and didn't want to pretend to care anymore. A week wasn't going to make a difference," Agatha repeated the same thing she had told her mom so many years before.

"That's not what I remember. I remember you went to school that morning, and then you left. Your friend, Dayle, asked where you had gone, and I said you were at school, but she said you never came to class," Buzz said.

"It's been a few years. I can't remember all the details," Agatha lied. There were just too many sisters in this little room asking her questions she didn't want to answer.

"Stop it, Agatha. Why did you quit school?" Harper asked again. As the oldest, she was always in charge of the interrogations. It was a job Agatha longed for.

"Was it because of Chris?" Lucy asked carefully.

Agatha was silent under the pressure, too silent.

"I'll take that as a yes," Buzz said with a smirk before pushing Agatha toward Lucy and sliding under the covers herself. Now there were three sisters leaning against the headboard, focused on Agatha. Somehow, Agatha knew that none of them would be her ally in this interrogation.

"No," Agatha deflected again.

"Yes. Tell." Harper pinched her leg, hard.

Pulling her leg to her chest she then admitted, "We danced at a party, and his friends made fun of me."

"Why would they make fun of you? Wouldn't his friends make fun of him?" Lucy asked.

She glared at her sister. "I am the artsy weirdo, Lucy. Not him."

"But they were his friends, so they were making fun of him for being with you. He was their target. Besides, his friends making fun of you isn't his fault," Harper said as she frowned at her.

"It doesn't matter." Agatha pulled her other leg up so that Harper couldn't pinch that one either.

"So one dance and poof, he's an asshole." Buzz made a hand motion like something exploded.

"Yes."

"Liar. What else happened?" Harper stated, inching her hand toward Agatha's feet.

"Nothing," Agatha said, trying to move her feet farther from her sister's pinchy fingers.

Harper stopped moving her hands and stared at her little sister for a moment, then stated in excitement, "You had sex with him. At the party?"

"No," Agatha lied badly.

"No wonder he poofed into an asshole," Buzz said, ignoring her.

"Was he your first?" Lucy asked with interest.

"Not talking about it," Agatha stated.

"Okay, so he was her first. It must have been at that party, and he was bad at it. Really bad," Lucy stated, nodding with enthusiasm.

"He wasn't bad," Agatha admitted before slapping her hand to her mouth. Suddenly, she was not very good at keeping her own secrets.

"How did he poof into an asshole then?" Buzz asked.

"He said that he wanted to date me. Nothing was set up, but we were going to be a couple," Agatha admitted the truth. Even to her, it sounded childish, but she had been a child when it happened.

"Yup, that's an asshole thing to do. That's why I didn't date high schoolers in high school," Lucy told the group with a giggle.

Harper turned to her. "Yes, you did, all the time."

"The poof, Agatha?" Buzz turned back to her.

"On Monday, he was talking to his friends, and they were asking about me. They heard we were together, and he told them I was—" She stopped. She didn't want to hear the words again.

"What?" Lucy pulled her closer to her.

"That I was good enough to fuck, but he would never date me." Agatha let the tears fall at the words that had destroyed her years before, words that still hung between them. Because no matter what happened between them over the last few months, they had never been on a date. Everything that had happened had been behind closed doors.

CHAPTER THIRTY-FOUR

By morning there were more cars in front of Agatha's house. He saw a Land Rover and the white Jeep, so he knew it must be Lucy and Harper. Once again, Chris decided to go over to see if Agatha would talk to him. His morning call to her went unanswered, as had his one the night before.

In the house, he headed for the voices in the kitchen. Harper was the first to notice him. She was elbows deep in the bowl of something slimy and brown and was not happy to see him at all.

"Get out of here, asshole," she spat out as she pulled a piece of something from the bowl and slammed it on the baking pan in front of her. Splattering herself with the slime as she did it.

"You heard her," Lucy said as she peeled potatoes.

"Did you talk to her?" he demanded It looked like everybody was in a bad mood today.

"Yes, and you are a fucking asshole. Leave." Lucy actually through a potato at his head, a whole potato.

"Can I at least know *why* I'm an asshole?" He put up his arms to fend off another flying vegetable.

"Something about my sister not being good enough for your

friends!" Harper reached into the bowl, and he hoped she wasn't in the throwing mood as well.

"I messed up! I was eighteen! I didn't know her address, and she never came back to school so that I could apologize." This time he let a potato hit him in the chest in hopes that the chicken Harper was mixing didn't come his way.

"So you admit you said it. Did you mean it?" Lucy demanded, another potato in her hand.

"No! I liked her for years. She was the one who didn't notice me. We weren't friends or anything, but I knew her and liked her," he admitted, and this time, no potato came his way.

"Prove it," Harper said.

"How?" he asked. It wasn't like he had anything in writing.

"Anything," Lucy said, tossing a potato in the air and catching it.

"Okay. When we were in the fifth grade, she had a Smurf backpack, and I wrote my initials on it in blue. I didn't think it would be so obvious since I wrote in blue marker, but it was. She never knew it was me who did it." He shrugged. It wasn't as if they would believe him, and the backpack was in a landfill somewhere by now.

Harper quickly went to the sink and washed her hands. "Why did you write your initials on it?"

"Because we had the same initials. I was going to write CL + CL but accidentally wrote CAL. I didn't know her middle name and chickened out on writing the rest." He watched the blonde leave the room, still drying her hands.

"Okay, what else?" Lucy asked, not caring that her sister had left.

"I was going to ask her to the big fall fifth-grade dance but also chickened out on that," Chris said, wishing he had not been such an idiot back then. He wouldn't be standing there trying to prove he had feelings for Agatha if he had just not been so scared then.

Harper rushed back into the kitchen and tossed a blue bag on the table and said, "Prove it."

Looking down at the bag, he actually questioned whether he had done what he remembered doing. After all, it had been over half a lifetime ago. Grabbing the bag, he flipped it over and was relieved his younger self had made such a bold statement.

Pointing to the letters, Chris wondered why this was important. He didn't even know if Agatha ever knew what he'd written. A few weeks later, she'd come to school with a red backpack. He had never seen the blue one again. Until now.

"Right here." He pointed the letters out, still just as visible as when he had written them.

Lucy picked it up and kind of squinted at it and asked, "Is he right?"

"Yes, but I didn't need the backpack to prove it. The bag was mine. I beat the tar out of her for writing on it after she swore she didn't. Agatha can't not draw on things. But in my defense, CAL are also her initials, just not the correct order." Harper plunged her hands back into the bowl of slime.

"Did you talk to her?" he asked once again, hoping that this was proof enough to get past these two gatekeepers. He wanted to talk to Agatha, not her sisters. He wanted to prove to her that he'd always liked her, not just now.

"Yes, and you are an asshole," Lucy said, going back to her peeling.

"I know that, but I need to talk to her and explain that I love her."

"She thinks once your friends know about her, you'll dump her again," Harper stated, slapping another chicken into the slime.

"No, I want to marry her." It was the truth. It had just taken her leaving to get him to admit how much he wanted her and for how long.

"What?" Harper asked, dropping a chicken on her shoe. She kicked it off and looked at the slimy thing.

"I never want to be without her. I want her and Poppy in my life forever."

"But Poppy isn't your kid." Harper looked at her sister warily. Tough crowd.

"I don't care; she is Agatha's kid, and I knew the night she brought Poppy home that if I wanted Agatha, I had to take Poppy too. I knew I wanted Agatha, so accepting the kid was easy. It doesn't hurt that she looks just like her gorgeous mother," Chris said.

Both women were staring at him like he had grown another head. Did they not think he would want the baby? Did they think that low of him?

"So, she thinks I care what my friends think? That it would change my feelings for her?" he asked.

"Yes," Lucy admitted, turning from her sister finally.

"Does she still work for you? Can you get her to work for you?" he asked the two.

"We can." Harper crossed her arms.

"Then I want to hire you," he stated. An idea started forming in his mind.

"When?" Harper pulled her hands away and looked at her slimy shirt and jeans as if she had forgotten how dirty her hands were.

"I need a week," he said. "Call me when you have an open date. Serve anything or nothing. I don't care. I just want her there."

Chris hurried out of the house. He was on a mission, a mission to get the love of his life back.

CHAPTER THIRTY-FIVE

Saturday morning dawned like any other, except they had gathered at Harper's, they were not eating leftovers, and nobody was in their pajamas. Oh, and the fact that there were three husbands in the living room.

Sadly, all combined, the breakfast felt completely different and completely off. Today there were four babies present, three of which were in the living room; only Poppy was welcome in the kitchen. Agatha assumed it was because she was a girl and not because they were treating Agatha differently because her baby's father was not there.

Tearing a muffin apart and putting it on the highchair for Poppy, Agatha let the conversation flow around her. Her daughter was trying to grab the chunks from her as fast as she could put them down, stopping only when her cheeks were packed full. Agatha put the muffin down and proceeded to pull muffin chunks from her mouth. Her kid had a lot of her daddy in her.

"I've got you down for Saturday night, Agatha. We need you," Lucy said from the table.

"I can't; I have a kid." Agatha pointed out. Maybe they would even be home by then. Chrisless, but at least home. His house had to be done soon.

"Buzz will watch her. She needs the practice and she is useless to us. You, on the other hand, we need." Lucy tried to ignore her own son crying in the living room with his father but was failing.

"Do you realize how many times I worked for you two when I was pregnant? Not once did I complain. Not once," Agatha argued.

"Bull! You were constantly complaining. You complained at every event, pregnant or not. Actually, you probably complained less when you were pregnant. I'm putting you on the schedule," Harper said.

"I don't want to."

"Too bad, you're needed. Wear something pretty." Harper smirked as they didn't have a dress code for their employees.

"I will not. And I want to be the first to leave," Agatha demanded, knowing there was no way out of this.

"I will put you down for clean-up," Lucy said with a grin until her baby cried again, which tore her attention away from the kitchen.

"Where's the event at?"

"The J," Harper answered for the distracted Lucy.

"Swanky," Agatha said, getting enough out of Poppy's cheeks for her baby to start filling them again. One of Harper's goals had been to become the in-house caterer at The J, but they had found it was too much work when they had finally gotten the contract. Now she and Lucy could work there anytime they wanted to. It was a high-end establishment.

"Oh, it is," Lucy agreed as she went to check on her baby.

"So, are husbands now invited if you have a baby, forcing us who don't have a baby to find one so we can bring our husbands?" Mabel asked.

Sera patted her hand. "Yes, honey. Baby first, and then you can bring Cliff."

"Totally unfair," Mabel grumbled.

"I agree with. Maby. It is unfair," Harper stated. Her man wouldn't be there if they weren't eating at her house.

"Pop out a spawn, and you too can bring your husband," Buzz said, patting her huge belly.

"Not ready yet. Cliff is enough of a kid." Mabel laughed.

"I'm just not ready yet, period. I like sex and sleep too much," Harper stated nonchalantly, then looked at her mom and blushed.

Agatha loved that every once in a while, it snuck up on her sister that she was married to Sera's twin brother.

"Sex is how you get kids, Harper, so you better watch out," Sera replied, not noticing Harper's reaction to the words.

Lucy brought in the sad baby boy, and Agatha watched her sit back down. As she arranged the baby on her lap, Lucy nodded in agreement. He was still in a gray pajama set and looked very upset with the crowd. Agatha couldn't tell Lucy's twins apart yet. In time she would, but until then, she was just calling them both baby. Not Luke and Owen.

"Not if you are careful." Maby took her nephew's hand in hers and shook it.

"I think there are a few 'carefuls' that went awry in this room," Sera answered with a grin.

"Harsh, Mom," Agatha said, once again pulling muffin from Poppy's mouth.

"I was thinking more about me." Sera shrugged and ran a hand over Violet's hair.

"I think that means me too," Emma suddenly said from the corner of the room where she had been hiding since getting there. Standing up in anger, she left for the safety of the living room.

"My first mistakes are always my best mistakes," Sera called after her oldest.

Harper leaned back in her chair and asked, "Violet, do you have an invisible friend?"

The little girl looked up at her oldest sister and said, "Not anymore."

"Did Mom chase him away?" Lucy asked once she had started to nurse the baby under a cover.

Violet looked from Harper to Lucy and then to her mom. "Yes."

Two sets of eyes turned on Agatha, who in turn, glared back at them. Neither said anything, but both wanted to. Ignoring them, she let herself be consumed by taking care of her baby, letting herself enjoy the task she had never thought she would get to do, but one she found herself enjoying more every day.

"Why haven't you ever said anything about her?" Mabel asked in interest.

"Because they are *my* friend!" Violet stated and crossed her arms in anger at her sister.

"Sorry for asking." Mabel let it drop.

Agatha wondered what all the talk about invisible friends was about. It wasn't like Violet had ever told her about one, but she wasn't quizzing the kid about it. With Violet, you had let her tell you when she wanted to tell. It wasn't like she didn't talk about almost everything all the time.

Within an hour, Sera and Harrison had taken their now three kids home, and Lucy had bundled up her two. Mabel and Buzz had left quickly because they still could with no kids in the world yet.

Harper was cleaning the kitchen as Agatha wiped down the high-chair that Harper had purchased for Poppy and all the other babies who would need it in the family. Finding the broom, she started sweeping up the crumbs from the floor. Kaine had taken Poppy to show her the toy selection in the living room.

"You don't have to sweep, Ag. Kaine can do that later." Harper giggled, Kaine paid people to do his sweeping. And Harper was in charge of them as mistress of the house, which was what she called herself.

"Poppy made the mess, so I can clean it for you," Agatha argued.

"Go ahead then, clean it all." Harper dropped her dishrag and went and sat at the still messy table.

"I will since you're now a lazy socialite," Agatha teased.

"Can I ask you a serious question and not have you just answer with 'fuck off'?" Harper asked as she crossed her arms.

"I really like to say fuck off." Agatha grinned, stopping her sweeping.

"You do. But seriously, can I?" Harper never talked like this. Agatha figured she must want to talk about Chris. She knew her sisters had spoken to him.

Leaning the broom against the counter, Agatha sat down near her sister. "Go ahead."

From out of nowhere, Harper asked, "Did you miscarry a baby the day Violet was born?"

She knew her face went pale. She could hear the blood rushing away from her body. Swallowing, she had no answer for the question —none that she wanted her sister to know about. It had been nine years and had never come up. There was no reason for Harper to bring it up now. How would Harper even have found out about it?

She tried to dodge. "Why do you ask?"

"I heard something about it."

"From who?" Agatha asked.

"Violet," Harper admitted.

Agatha let out her breath. Violet didn't know what had happened. Violet was just a kid, barely born as it had unfolded.

"She's just a kid making stuff up," Agatha assured her sister.

"She said her invisible friend is your lost baby," Harper pressed, eyes glued to her face.

If there had been any blood left in her body, it was gone now, replaced by ice and cold. It took everything in her to not shake at the chill.

"Kids," she said lamely.

"She said he was born the same day she was and that his name is Jet," Harper said very slowly, letting each word sink in.

The shaking was uncontrollable. Her sister had to see it, but she didn't comment. She just took Agatha's hand in hers and held it tight. Agatha knew that Harper knew the answer was yes, but Agatha couldn't say the words.

"I am not going to ask why you didn't tell anyone, because you keep a lot inside. But I want you to let someone in there. You can't do it all by yourself. I think we know now that if you hadn't gotten pregnant with Poppy, you might have died by now. You needed to have her, and that changed everything for you. When she was gone, you didn't go back to being out-of-control Agatha. You just stayed the Agatha we love. Maybe you and Chris were meant to be apart for a while. He had to do the football thing, fail, and then find out he was more than a football player. And you needed to find yourself with your art."

Harper didn't let go of her hand, but Agatha couldn't bring herself to look up. Her words were settling in Agatha's mind. Was she right that they were different people than they were eighteen months before or even in high school? Was it unfair of her to judge him on his actions from back then and not by who he had been when they were together now?

"And then when Poppy was conceived, neither of you were ready for that. But now you are. You two are so ready to do this together, but the past is getting in the way. He is lost without you, and you are lost without him." Harper let their hands go and pushed her chair back, leaving her little sister alone to think.

Was her sister right? That they hadn't been ready to be together, that they didn't know what they wanted, much less who they wanted to be? Each of them had a road to walk down before they could meet up again and make it work.

CHAPTER THIRTY-SIX

THE REST of the week had gone by without a single sighting of Agatha. But the few times her sisters came to her house, they did willingly talk to him. They also started using his name and not just calling him whatever they wanted to. Those names usually weren't very nice, but it seemed now that they were treating him differently.

On Wednesday, he had talked to his brother and admitted that he had failed in flipping the house. He had no idea what he was doing and didn't want to do remodeling anymore. He also told his brother that he was going to do what he should have months before: he would start working in the family business. Even though Chris had never shown any interest in the business, Carter had willingly let him into the fold. He had even given him an office and was letting him choose what he wanted to do with his days, as long as it was insurance-related, that is.

In the meeting, he had told his brother about Agatha. Carter had just grinned at him and asked if she was the little dark-haired girl who he had teased all the time at school. It seemed he might be the kid from kindergarten after all. Or it might have been just a coincidence. That was until his sister confirmed that he had gotten in trouble that entire year for being mean to a little dark-haired girl with a lisp.

Chris had invited both of his siblings and their spouses to the party he was planning on Saturday night. He also invited his mom, who declined right away, which wasn't a surprise. Agatha wasn't part of the right social circle, after all, which was perfect for Chris. He just hoped Agatha would be a part of *his* circle soon.

The rest of the week was spent calling, texting, and emailing four hundred people who had the privilege of graduating on the same day as him. Though only a dozen were his friends back then, he made special effort to get everyone there. Many didn't remember him, and some even said they weren't coming because it was him, but he was doing whatever it took to win Agatha back.

There had only been a few people he'd contact that remembered Agatha at all. One had been her close friend who had lost contact with Agatha when high school was over. Another had been one of his closest friends, who had admitted that he was surprised Chris would even fall for someone like her. Which made him want to disinvite the man, except this was exactly who he needed to invite. People who he had spent his youth trying to impress. People who he didn't want to even associate with anymore.

The house was quiet, dark, and was starting to echo his own sad look with Agatha gone. But hopefully, she would be back soon. He was so lost in thought as he analyzed her house that he missed the woman walking up his front sidewalk.

"So, Cliff is buying this place for Maby?" Sera Dean asked, not even snarling at him. It was the first time she hadn't done it since he'd met her.

"Yes, it's a secret, though. I don't think he's told her yet," he informed Sera, in case she was planning on telling Maby. Cliff had sworn him to secrecy about the purchase when they had agreed upon a price.

"Oh, he told her. He really can't keep a secret from his lady love," Sera said, using was the same words Cliff had used to call his wife, his lady love. Sera stopped in front of Chris, looking at him closely.

Finally, Sera came right out and asked. "The girls say you're in love with Agatha. Are you?"

"I am. I want to marry her. Should I be asking you for permission?" he asked, standing up straight. After all this time, he needed to start getting on this woman's good side.

"No, you should ask her. I let my kids do what they want to do," she said with a smile as she turned to look at Agatha's house across the street, the house she had raised her kids in. At least her older kids.

His eyebrow shot up in question. That was not the impression he had ever got from her. To him, she was a mama bear, and he had gotten too close to her cub. She had taken more swipes at him than he cared to think about.

"When you're not involved, that is," she relented and turned back to him. "But you were.... You didn't see her after everything that happened with you back then. I did. I never wanted to see her that way again. I still don't. So, if you aren't in it forever, I would like you to leave now."

Sera stood her ground and crossed her arms, daring him to say he was just playing with Agatha's emotions.

But Chris wasn't scared. He was so in love with Agatha he couldn't breathe when she wasn't around.

"I want her forever, and everything that entails. I want to help her raise Poppy and have more kids of our own. I want to be there every day. I just want to tell her face-to-face, but I can't find her," he promised, wishing he could make the same promises to her daughter. He knew he would, and soon. But soon wasn't coming quick enough for him.

"Good, because I will break your other knee if you ever hurt Agatha again," Sera said. He wondered if she actually knew which knee he had broken, but he didn't want to find out. Her eyes looked like she knew.

Chris smirked at her bravado. "I'll remember that." He loved that despite what she said, he knew she would always be a mama bear for Agatha. The woman he loved needed everyone she could get in her corner.

CHAPTER THIRTY-SEVEN

It had been weeks since Agatha had worn the starched white shirt and not-so-flattering black pants that Harper insisted all the waitstaff wear. Tonight, it was Agatha and sisters, Frankie and Louisa, that were working the event. Harper had given her pep talk and then handed out trays of hors d'oeuvres to the group to pass around.

"Why do you hate me?" Agatha asked her older sister.

"I love you the best. You can't lick them if they're slimy shrimp." Harper shoved the platter into her hands. The cocktail sauce glittered in the fluorescent lights in their tiny bowls.

"I quit," Agatha stated loudly.

"You can't," Lucy reminded her. Agatha tried to quit every time she worked.

"One day, you won't see me again," said Agatha. She hoped it sounded like a curse.

"One day, you will be happy to work for me," Harper replied, touching her hair. "Just like these two." She motioned to her newest recruits, or as Agatha called them, suckers. Neither had ever worked for Harper before, and neither seemed overly excited about it. Okay, Louisa was excited, but Frankie seemed as pissed about it as Agatha.

It seemed when short on waitstaff, Harper would rather pay for plane tickets for the two sisters to fly in from another state than to pay strangers. Agatha wondered how much money Harper and Lucy were throwing away tonight. Then again, they were both married to billionaires and worked for fun, so money wasn't a real worry for them anymore.

"This is so exciting!" Louisa said beside her in a whisper.

"Give it like a minute, and it'll be awful," Agatha told her with a grin.

"I don't even need a minute," Frankie said, checking to make sure her blue hair was tucked neatly in the bun on her head.

The sisters couldn't be more different. Then again, they were actually Lovelys, so being different was a given. Louisa was a goody two-shoes, and Frankie, the blue-haired sister, was as wild as any Lovely had been at twenty-two.

Agatha hoped that they would visit them more often because she didn't know them well and thought that they would get along. Maybe once she moved back home, she would invite them to move in with her. It would be nice to have a house full of Lovelys again, except she wasn't ready to return yet. Maybe in time.

Her heart still ached when she thought about Chris, and she thought about him constantly. For days she has wanted to go back to him, to forgive him and hope that he would forgive her. But suddenly, her sisters were no longer talking about him or telling her about him hanging around. Was it because he was over her? Had she gotten her wish, and he realized she wasn't worth it? She was afraid to find out.

"Okay, smile everyone and look happy," Lucy said to the three sisters.

Following Frankie into the room, Agatha started her usual mindless circling. It had been years since she cared what the function she was working was all about. She didn't see a bride and groom, so it probably wasn't a wedding, which was a plus. Weddings always lasted forever.

After a full circle, she recognized three of the attendees. They had graduated from high school with her. One had been the homecoming queen, and another was Dayle, who had been her best friend those last few months of school. Both had acknowledged her with a nod or a wave. The homecoming queen looked exactly the same, but Dayle didn't. Dayle had gone from total goth to total sophistication in nine years. Her dress was form-fitting like it had been sewn just for her and in a perfect shade to complement her dark blond hair. Dayle's hair had been as dark as Agatha's in high school.

After leaving school that day, she never spoke to Dayle again, just closed that door of her life with Dayle on the other side. For a moment, she wanted to rush to her and see how her life was going but held back. She was just the staff tonight, after all.

The third person she recognized had been the biggest surprise. It had been Savannah, Chris's high school flame. She was prettier now than she'd been in high school, much nicer looking than the homecoming queen. She wondered if she and Chris were still friends? Agatha was sure he wouldn't have looked her way if Savannah had still been around.

After another loop around the room, she began picking out more faces that she hadn't seen in years, their names ones she no longer knew. But they were there. Some were in jeans, and some were in suits and dresses. She realized that the event had to be a class reunion for her graduating class. And joy upon joy, she was there as a waiter for the catering company. Not as an author or artist, but a worker for the event, someone who hadn't even been invited. Or maybe she had. Maybe the invitation was just at her house, which she hadn't been to in weeks.

So far, she hadn't seen Chris, but if the entire class had been invited, so had he. After all, he was Mr. Popularity back then. No way would they not invite him.

Her third trip around the room found her hors d'oeuvres more popular, and her tray was almost empty when she slipped into the kitchen. Usually, Harper had a tray ready, but this time she was not ready and was just beginning to fill little bowls with cocktail sauce. Which was fine since Agatha didn't want to be out on the floor anyway. How many of them knew it was her and that she wasn't invited, just working there? More than enough to make her want to hide in here.

Watching Harper work, Agatha decided she wasn't going to mention it was her class reunion out there; it would just make Harper sad that Agatha wasn't invited. It was bothering Agatha more then she liked to admit. She wanted to be a guest. She wanted to be included.

After their talk that morning, she had wanted to avoid this evening but hadn't wanted Harper to think she was avoiding her, which would have been true. She never wanted to have that conversation with her sisters again.

"Here you go. I love you. You know that, right?" Harper said, handing her the tray.

"I love you too, Harps, but if you ever use these cups again...." Agatha made a cutting motion against her throat and picked up the tray. With a fake smile, she headed back out to serve food to her former classmates.

As she started circling the room, the light piano music coming from the overhead speaker abruptly cut off. Her fake smile became real as she wondered if they would have to call a sound guy to fix the music or if it was an easy fix. Either way, a mess-up that wasn't her fault was fun.

That was when she saw Chris, looking handsome as fuck in a tux. His curls were combed to his head, and he was looking right at her. Someone took the tray she was surely dropping from her hand. She had nowhere to run, nowhere to go to get away from him. Not that she really wanted to.

As the seconds ticked by, they stared at each other, neither one moving. The music had started back up, but now it wasn't the piano music that had played before.

When the first whispered line, of "Hero" began to play, her heart and breath stopped completely. Agatha couldn't believe the song was actually playing. It had to be all in her head, and she was going fucking nuts. The world didn't stop for someone like her, but if it had, this was the best dream she had ever had.

Chris had already stepped close and was pulling her into his arms as the next line played, "Would you dance, if I asked you to dance?" His hands slid down to her hips and encircled her waist.

In a whisper, he asked as if she wasn't already in his arms, "Will you dance with me, Agatha?"

Trying to control her emotions, she could only nod and slide her hands up his chest and encircled his neck. How could he still feel and smell the exact same as he when they were together? God, how she had missed him.

As the song continued, she wondered if he remembered the song that they danced to that night or if it had just been a good guess. A tear rolled down her cheek. She knew he remembered, just like she had. His arms slid across her back and pulled her closer to him. They had ceased dancing, now content to hold each other tight.

Quietly in her ear, he started singing the words to her, the words begging her to forgive him and to stay with him forever. Her heart melted as she pressed herself further into his warmth, wanting the moment to never end.

He stopped singing to say, "I love you, Agatha. Stay with me forever. I want to spend my life being your hero."

His words were everything she had ever wanted to hear from him, but far more than she deserved after how she had treated him. She should've been apologizing to him and begging for his forgiveness; instead, he had made everything around them happen. For her. All to prove that he had changed, that he wanted her no matter who knew. But she needed to prove to him she had changed also.

"Chris," she started but couldn't say more through her tears.

He kissed a tear away. "I want to get down on one knee and propose, but I can't let you go yet. I asked everyone in our class to come tonight so that they could all see me propose to you. So, they would all know I love you. I messed it up all those years ago, I don't want to do that again."

With his words, she remembered she was in the middle of a function as a waiter. Looking at the crowd, she saw semi-familiar faces watching them, but also all of her sisters and her mom. Then she caught sight of their husbands and Lucy and Harper, who had ventured out of the kitchen. She realized they had all been in on this.

Jonas walked up to them and handed her Poppy, who was wearing a little black dress with black tights to match her parent's outfits. She instantly snuggled into their tight embrace, where she belonged. As a threesome, they didn't dance through the rest of the song as it played. Chris sang to Agatha and Poppy the words of promise again.

"Will you marry me, Agatha Christie Lovely? Will you let me be your hero?" he asked when the song ended.

"Yes," she whispered. Even though she spoke softly, Christ still heard, picking her up and kissing her as they turned in circles and the song started again. She thought that the crowd cheered but couldn't be sure because Chris was kissing her, and that consumed all of her senses.

The kiss ended, and Chris called out, "I'm taking them home, Harper."

"Car seat's in your car!" Jonas yelled back as Chris carried her and Poppy from the room to cheers from more than just her family.

Even better, nobody was laughing at her. At them.

CHAPTER THIRTY-EIGHT

IT TOOK TWICE AS LONG as it should have to get them the mile to Agatha's home, mostly because he couldn't stop touching her, kissing her, and telling her he loved her. Also, Poppy's car seat was impossible to figure out.

After pulling in front of her house, he saw everything was in place liked he'd wanted. Her sisters were suckers for a happy ending. Now that he had won them over, they were friendly.

The house was completely lit up, and there were flower petals over every floor from the first floor to the third. White roses on the first floor, red on the second, and Poppy petals on the third. The house smelled like a flower shop, which covered the closed-up smell it had begun to sport.

"What did you do?" she asked from his arms as he carried her into the house with Poppy's car seat dangling from his arm. Never was he so glad he had spent years working out.

"Your sisters and Sera might have helped a little. It seems Sera's sister owns a flower shop and had some really good ideas about flowers," he admitted. There had been some more wild ideas that he had vetoed, but he knew that Agatha would love the surprise. Even if she wouldn't admit it.

"What?" she demanded with a smile.

"Don't be mad at them." He kissed her nose that she had wrinkled at the thought of her sisters' involvement.

"We'll see how I feel tomorrow," she joked with a smile.

"I have a few things to do before we get to making you feel good," he said and put her on the floor and the car seat on the couch.

Chris easily freed Poppy from her car seat, which she was more cooperative for. Kissing her head, Chris snuggled her close because he had missed the little thing a lot over the last few weeks. He turned to her mom and pulled a ring from his pocket.

The ring was big and bulky, made of gold with a large red stone in the center. "I want to give you my class ring to wear, so everyone knows you're mine." He liked that she smiled at his words. She took the ring and tried it on her thumb, but it was too big. Chris laughed.

Reaching back into his pocket, he pulled out a smaller ring. This one had one red stone and thirteen smaller diamonds around it. "The ruby is your birthstone. The smaller stones represent each year we were in school together."

She looked at the ring as he slid it on her finger. Her eyes met his, and she said, "But we were only in school together since the third grade."

"No, we started kindergarten together. I can show you the yearbook to prove it. You were Agatha that year. In the third grade, I remember everyone called you Chrissy, I don't know why."

"I couldn't say the 'st' sound," she admitted.

"I want you to wear this ring so that you remember my promise to love you forever and marry you one day. When we're both ready." He kissed her forehead as he slid it on her finger, which was a bit loose.

"I was supposed to put this on your finger before we left the party, but I couldn't let you go." He held up another ring, a single diamond completely circled by smaller diamonds. Pulling the ruby ring he had just slid onto her finger, he moved it to the finger right beside it, where it fit. He then slid the new ring on her ring finger. "Agatha Christie Lovely, will you marry me? As soon as fucking possible, please?"

"Yes," she repeated her answer she'd given him at The J.

"Can I move in with you until then?" he asked, shifting Poppy in his arms.

"I don't know where else you would go. Have you bought another house to destroy?" She giggled, and he decided he loved the sound.

"I'm done destroying houses. From now on, I'll be working with Carter at Lowell Insurance," he admitted. Maybe he should have talked to her about it, but it was done.

"You? In insurance? I guess we all have hidden talents." Pulling him to her, she kissed him.

Chris winked. "Once your princess is sleeping, I'll show you some hidden talents."

"I don't even know what all is here." She looked at the stairs.

"Everything. Jonas and Buzz brought all of Poppy's things back. Either you said yes, and we came here, or you said and no, and I walked away. You were coming home tonight." He ran his hand over her cheek.

"Did you think you would be here tonight?" she asked as she started up the stairs.

"I had hopes. Otherwise, you would be spending days cleaning up flower petals alone." He followed her as she went, admiring her ass in her black pants.

At the top of the stairs, she took Poppy from his arms and went into the room she had made up for her weeks before. The baby's clothes had all been returned to the closet and dresser.

Watching her change the baby, he realized he had missed so much. Before, she had been hesitant when taking off Poppy's clothes. Now she had done it so often she didn't even think about it, maneuvering the little body with ease and putting a pair of yellow pajamas on her.

"What color are her pajamas?" he asked from the doorway.

"Daffodil," she said, handing the baby to him. "Can I change, or are you dreaming of ripping this gorgeous waitress outfit off me?"

"I can rip anything off you, gorgeous." He moved aside so that she could go to her room.

"Then I better not pick my favorite shirt." She walked past him, unbuttoning the white shirt as she went.

"I wish I could remember that night in the hotel, when I must have ripped this off of you." He watched her pull the shirt down and toss it into the dirty clothes hamper.

"I won't tell you about it; it'll just depress you." Grinning, she grabbed a T-shirt from her drawer. It said nothing; it was just a blue shirt. Chris smiled. He liked that he could rip this shirt off her, because if it had any writing on it, she wouldn't let him.

"Because it was so good or bad?" His eyes were on her body as she shimmied out of her black pants.

"It was good," she admitted, grabbing for sweatpants in her dresser.

"It's always been good." He leaned against the door, loving that she was his now.

Tossing the sweatpants on the bed, she took Poppy from him, hugged the baby to her, and sat on the bed. Poppy sucked on her thumb as he watched Agatha pull all three rings off her fingers and toss them on the mint green strip of the comforter. Then she looked at them, slowly rocking the baby in her arms.

"There are things you should know before you give me these back." Her eyes looked at him and then back to the ring pile.

With his heart in his throat he asked, "What?"

She picked up the rings and laid them in a line, a few inches between each one. Picking up the class ring, she said, "In high school during that party when we had sex, it was my first time. I never told you that."

"I kind of figured that out," he admitted.

"I, um, got pregnant that night, but I miscarried at four months. It messed me up for a while. I had sex with a lot of guys for a few years. I partied and drank and did a lot of messed-up shit. I didn't get my life back on track for years. Most of the time, I didn't even try." She pushed the ring farther from her.

Grief raced through him. How had Violet known? How had he not even considered that he was the cause of her pain when there was even a hint she was pregnant back then? Going through that sort of trauma would make anyone act out, and Agatha had just done what she thought she needed to erase the pain. But it couldn't be erased; it could only be lessened. And she had done it all without him.

Crouching down by the bed, he pushed the ring back in line. "I wasn't a boy scout myself. I played football and let everything else slide. I was that guy, and I regret letting that happen. That night in the hotel room wasn't the only one I can't remember. We both went through some bad years."

Pushing the promise ring with the large ruby on it, she said, "That night in the hotel room, I knew you were too drunk to really consent, but I wanted you again. Just one more time. The next morning, I missed an appointment with a publishing house. I sabotaged myself."

"I try not to think I was the biggest asshole in that hotel room that night. I wanted you, and I took you. And I was left not even knowing what happened." He pushed the ring back in the line. Then he picked it up and put it back on her hand, where it belonged.

Her arms tightened around Poppy's still body, and he heard her take a deep breath and push the engagement ring forward. "Poppy is yours."

Unable to stop his smile, he picked up the ring and placed it on her finger where he had first put it, where it belonged. "I know. When you said you were Christie, I knew she was mine. I felt like she was mine from day one. I *wanted* her to be mine the moment you said she was yours."

Not that he would let himself do anything but hope they had created this amazing child, that something good had come from them just once in the past. But knowing the truth made his heart sore. He had a daughter. He had a daughter with the woman he loved.

"Do you hate me? I gave her away. I just gave her to strangers." A tear slid from her eye and disappeared into Poppy's dark hair.

"No, you did what you thought was best for her. We weren't ready yet, either of us. Now we are, and we have her, and we have each other. We're together, all three of us. And we'll have more." He caught the next tear and wiped it away with his thumb.

Every word he said was true. He had loved the baby since day one, even when he had no idea who the father was. When Agatha had said she was Christie, he had wondered if it was possible that she was his. There were little things about Poppy that reminded him of himself. That Agatha was finally admitting it made his heart soar. He had a daughter, a perfect daughter with the perfect woman. And they were together. How they came to be a family was a long, winding road, but it was over, and they were family. Never again would they be separated.

"More? As in more kids?" She looked up at him with a raised eyebrow.

"At least another one, maybe four more. All girls and wild like their aunts. Poppy has a lot to live up to as a female in the Lovely family." He ran his hand lightly down his daughter's back.

"She's also a Lowell," Agatha said.

"She's a Lovely Lowell. Poppy Agatha Lovely Lowell." Taking Poppy from Agatha, he wrapped her in his arms and said her name again, making the baby smile.

"Not Agatha," Agatha protested with a frown. "Poppy Seraphina Lovely Lowell."

"Then the next one we'll name Agatha." He leaned down and kissed her still wet cheek.

"Christopher," she said on a sigh.

"Agatha Christopher Lovely Lowell, we will have to get started right away," he said, making her laugh. "But first, we have to make you a Lowell. How soon can that be done?"

He didn't want to rush her. He knew how important a big wedding was to some people, but he didn't want to wait. He had waited long enough.

"Mom can have us married in three days." Agatha grinned with confidence.

"Monday or Tuesday?" he asked because that was sooner than he had ever expected. He had expected to wait a month or more. Probably more. Three days was perfect.

"Both," was all she answered and pulled him down into a kiss, a kiss that made him regret that his daughter was still awake.

"Now how soon can you get this one asleep? I need to see how many pillows I can make you destroy." He set the baby on the bed but grabbed her leg so that she didn't crawl to the edge and fall off.

"That might take time, Daddy." She smirked at him, still in her panties.

Groaning, he kissed her smart little mouth and turned his attention away from her and to his daughter. Once his daughter was sleeping, he would focus on her mom. After all, there were still pillows on the bed. A lot of them.

CHAPTER THIRTY-NINE

WAKING up in the early morning had started to feel normal even after years of going to bed as the sun came up. But Poppy didn't like Agatha's old routine and had been working at changing it since she had brought home. Agatha was willing to trade the old her for the new her. If the new Agatha had Poppy in it, that is.

Slipping on leggings and a T-shirt, she went into her daughter's bedroom, a room she hadn't been in weeks. Last night, it hadn't seemed to bother Poppy about being in the new location, but that had become normal for her also. But that old normal stopped today. This was their home, and they were staying.

Her daughter should have been inside the white crib, wide awake and waiting for her mom to come and get her, but it was empty. The pale pink sheets and blanket were cold to the touch.

"What the hell?" she mumbled and lifted the blankets in case she had missed the baby, but who missed a baby in a crib?

Panic engulfed her because she had just left Chris in bed. Who else would have removed the baby from her room? Turning, she saw a purple folder in the center of Poppy's changing table. Rushing over, she knew exactly what it was, but why was it there? What could it possibly say?

Opening it, she saw a type-written letter from none other than Sera Dean. As far as Agatha could tell, she had taken Poppy for the morning. It seemed she needed some grandma time with her newest grandchild. The letter went on to detail the legal rights of grandparents to see their children's kids. Agatha noticed there was nothing about kidnapping in it, but that was exactly what this was, kidnapping.

Taking the letter, she marched over to her own bedroom, where Chris was still sound asleep. His head was buried in the pile of pillows neither had had the energy to remove the night before. The sheet had slipped down to reveal his back, his gorgeous, manly, sexy, muscular back. It was mouthwatering from across the room.

He rolled over and groaned as she watched. She hoped that the sheet would slip a bit more. Their night of passion had been short since she was exhausted after a day with Poppy and working. She had a feeling she was getting old.

Shaking her head, Agatha walked into the room, waving the paper in her hand. "My fucking mother stole my baby!"

"You mean your mom took our baby so that you could sleep in?" he asked reasonably, as if reason played any part in Agatha's current emotions.

She waved the folder at him. "No! She says something about her legal rights as a grandma and that I need to be at her place at 10 a.m. You can tell she's married to a fucking lawyer." Poppy was his kid too! He should be just as concerned.

Jumping out of bed naked, he grabbed the paper from her and threw it on the ground. Picking her up, he said, "That means we have until ten."

"You're not understanding, Chris She took our kid!" Agatha half squealed as he tossed her onto the bed.

"Oh, I understand. I have you alone for another," he looked at the clock, "three hours."

"What more did you want to do with me that you haven't already done?" She giggled as he pulled off the leggings and panties she had so recently put on. She knew what he wanted: the same thing she did.

She would have to thank her stepmom for this time alone with Chris. It was the nicest way to start the day, but a simple phone call would have been better than a legal document and a stolen child.

"For one thing, we haven't made love yet today." He pushed her shirt over her head with just a little help from her. Because they were alone, and even if their relationship was new, she wasn't wasting precious alone time.

"Yes, yes we have." She couldn't stop smiling as he climbed into the bed and kissed up her leg.

He licked her inner thigh. "Not since I woke up. That makes it a new day. This is the first full day of our short, short engagement."

"I should be very upset with you about this marriage thing. You know I'm going to get roped into going dress shopping now. I wasn't thinking when I said yes." She groaned until his tongue circled her belly button, and pleasure shot straight to her core.

Her words stopped him completely just as he was about to kiss her stomach. Looking down, she saw the concern in his eyes. Concern that meant he was worried that she didn't want to marry him anymore.

Running her fingers through his curls, Agatha pulled him up her body and kissed him. Pulling away, she told him, "Chris, I want to be married to you, but getting married is a big hassle in this family. High Drama."

"Are you sure?" He looked down at her, his face inches from hers.

"Positive. I want to be your wife. I want to spend every day of my life with you." She lifted her hand so that she could look at the ring, which she loved. Both of them.

"Let's elope." He adjusted her arms so that they were over her head and ran his fingers over her arms, causing her to shiver.

"That will kill Sera," she admitted on a sigh, though it would have been perfect. Sera loved to plan weddings, and she was surely planning theirs right now. Even if neither the bride nor groom where there, it didn't matter. Sera knew what she wanted in a wedding. The actual bride didn't matter.

"How much of a wedding can she pull together in a few days?" He leaned down and nuzzled her neck, sucking on the spot he knew drove her crazy.

"Elaborate, very elaborate." She shivered, not only at what he was doing to her but how over the top the wedding could be.

"I'm not worried, because no matter what happens at the wedding, I get to marry you." He reached over her head and set a pillow by her head.

Grabbing the pillow in her hands, she looked at it in confusion. "What's this for?"

Nipping at her collarbone, he smiled and winked as he shimmied down her body. "Just something for you to hold on to."

"You know that was a one-time thing, right? That it will never happen again," she explained. He had been trying since their first time to recreate her pillow destruction, but it hadn't happened again, much to Chris's disappointment.

"Can't hurt to try again." He bit down gently on her scar, the one he never failed to give some attention to when they made love. One day, she might just tell him that he had bitten her that night so many months ago. That he had caused the scar. Just like the one on her head. Forever reminders of this man.

"Give it your all, Lowell," she said, shutting her eyes as his tongue licked up her leg. Her light grip on the pillow turned fierce as her world and body exploded under his touch.

By the time her body had stopped pulsating and quivering, she lay on his chest, just like he always positioned them after sex. She was nestled on his chest, and his arms wrapped around her. Opening her eyes, she was nearly blinded by the ear-to-ear smile covering his smug face. A smug face that was speckled with white flecks of fluff. He had succeeded in his goal. Agatha knew she should probably be mad, but she was too content for that right now. Maybe later.

At this rate, she was going to have to invest in more pillows—a lot more pillows.

CHAPTER FORTY

AGATHA WOULDN'T TELL him what the plan was, but he called his mom and family and requested that they come to Agatha's house and meet his fiancée and daughter. Since he hadn't actually talked to his sister or brother the night of the party, and Agatha hadn't at all, they were very eager to meet Agatha. His mom once again declined the offer. Once again, he didn't care. If she wouldn't make time for his family, he didn't need her in his family.

Within an hour, the house was completely full, with his family and Agatha's family there. Agatha and Cliff began immediately arguing in the backyard for a few minutes. When he asked about it later, Cliff had said it had been about property lines. But that had been when Carter and his wife had arrived, so he had to leave them to fight it out. He was sure that Agatha was winning the fight anyway.

Wearing a white "LUN" shirt, Agatha carried Poppy through the crowd. The little girl was in a frilly little dress in sunburst, not orange, or so he had been told.

Harper and Kaine came into the house, both carrying pans of something that smelled amazing. "Okay, Ag, we're having chicken and pork chops because I didn't have enough of the dish you were looking for. Luce is bringing the sides and desserts. P.S., there will be a bill for this. A very, very large bill."

"Just give it to Sera; she's paying," Agatha said to her sister and smiled a thank-you at her brother-in-law.

"Why am I paying? The mother of the bride does not pay for the rehearsal dinner," Sera argued as she tried to bounce her son to sleep. Agatha handed Poppy to Chris and took the baby from her. "Don't think I don't know that this is just an elaborate way for you to get out of going dress shopping today."

Yes, Agatha was supposed to have gone dress shopping after their amazing sex two days before, but Agatha had called in sick, and Sera had nearly cried on the phone. Then Agatha had admitted she just wanted some time with Chris, and her stepmom had given in, saying she would keep the baby for the rest of the day. Sera also hinted that her wedding dress might end up fitting Harper better than Agatha since her sister was trying them on for her. Dress shopping was happening no matter what.

"You caught me." Agatha bumped her mom with her shoulder and winked. She was surprisingly happy to go with her stepmom after lunch was finished.

Heading over to his family, he handed off Poppy to his sister. The baby was always happy to go to strangers. As a father, maybe he should be a little concerned about that,but Chris decided not to be. Poppy was perfect.

Cliff rushed in the door with an old man who seemed angrier than anything. He looked around the room and groaned at all the people gathered.

Cliff whistled loudly, and half the women yelled at him not wake the babies.

Agatha jumped on the couch and announced, "Thank you, everyone, for coming today. Chris and I are happy we can spend this special day with the ones we love."

"Special day?" Sera questioned from beside them.

Agatha turned to her and smiled. "We're getting married."

"Tomorrow," Sera reminded her. She had been planning their

wedding since the moment the engagement was announced, possibly before. Chris didn't even know what all the woman had in store for them the next day. All he knew was that they needed to be at the cathedral at 10 a.m.

"Today," Agatha corrected and jumped off the couch to stand by her mom. "Will you be a witness?"

"Of course, but it's tomorrow. I still have a lot to do." She smiled and tried to hug Agatha, who leaned away.

"Not this time. Just relax." Agatha took her stepmom's hand in hers.

Sera smiled and looked around the room. "But it's tradition, Agatha. I plan the weddings, and you girls just go along with it. From it, you get a gorgeous wedding and memories to last a lifetime." She stopped and then quickly added, "And a husband."

Agatha pulled the woman into a hug. "It was all a lie, Sera."

They were all married now, so there was no need to keep the truth from Sera anymore. It had always bothered her that Sera was never invited; she would have loved the late nights with little to no notice of what was happening. They had only kept it from her to spare her feelings since none of them wanted a big wedding. It was time to let the cat out of the bag.

"Agatha! Stop!" Harper yelled, though her next shout was muffled when her husband wrapped her into a hug and covered her mouth with his hand.

"Agatha, you snitch!" one of the twins shouted from behind him.

Agatha just kept hugging her stepmom and said, "Every one of them got married hours before the actual wedding. With only the family there. That's how everyone wanted to get married."

Agatha let Sera go and looked into her eyes. Even from across the room, he could tell the older woman was crying. Then her eyes darted to each of her married daughters and asked in a raspy voice, "Why wasn't I there?"

"Because you were planning the big one," Agatha said.

"But Maby and Cliff got married in the cathedral. It was gorgeous," Sera pointed out with tears in her eyes at the memory.

"Actually, it happened in their apartment at two in the morning," Buzz said from the corner of the couch, still pregnant and miserable.

"Harper and Kaine were married in their living room. It was a gorgeous day," Sera tried again.

"Same living room, only it was the middle of the night," Kaine said as he let his wife go finally.

"Lucy and Leo?"

"Six a.m. in the kitchen here at the house as she prepped the food Harper was supposed to be making. Lucy couldn't let her do it alone," Leo said as his wife tried to cover his mouth but failed.

"Buzzy?" She turned to her last daughter.

"In the middle of the night at the hotel." Louisa was grinning as she jumped in with the answer, as if she had been just waiting to tell what she knew.

"Do you know how much money was spent on those weddings? And time? All the time I wasted?" Sera demanded of the room.

"Yes, and they all tried to get out of it. They had plans, and you didn't let them happen. But I don't want to just go along with it, so the judge is here, and we are getting married right now," Agatha said with a smile.

"Now?" Sera sat down on the couch, looking lost.

Agatha sat down with her and hugged her. "Yes, right now, and you're going to be my witness. You and Chris's brother."

That was when Chris realized what was happening. This wasn't just Agatha's mom getting the surprise of a lifetime. It was also his wedding day, and he hadn't even known about it.

"Agatha, can I have a word with you?" he said and picked her up off the couch and threw her over his shoulder. Chris carried her into the empty kitchen where they could talk in peace.

In the kitchen, he sat her on the counter so that they were at eye level. "Did you forget to talk to me about this?"

"I knew you would say no, but then again, you wanted to get married ASAP," she argued, her dark eyes dancing.

"I thought this was an engagement party," he replied, pointing at the room full of people.

"Do you know what's even better than an engagement party? A wedding!" She threw her arms around him and kissed him.

Resting his forehead against hers, he said, "I thought you hated parties."

"I hate weddings, and you wanted to elope. Let's elope in our living room with our families." She wrapped her legs around him and clung to him.

Chris was starting to like her idea more and more. "But my mom and all our other guests are going to be at the cathedral tomorrow," he argued.

Sera ventured into the kitchen. "How about we do this one today and then the cathedral tomorrow for everyone else? I mean, think of who isn't here. Bex and Arabella aren't here. Chris's mom isn't here. Your lawyer, Aspen, isn't here. Leo's girls aren't even here. We can't have you getting married without any of them. Tomorrow they will be there."

"Mom," Agatha groaned into his chest.

"No, it could work. It will be beautiful, and we can still go get you a gorgeous dress for the wedding. And dresses for all your sisters since they're all bridesmaids. All eight of them. Good thing Chris is a football player; we needed more guys," Sera said, clapping her hands in excitement. "And I already have the top hats. I regretted not using them with Mabel, but I get to with you. Oh, and the doves. I know how much you loved the doves."

"That's defeating the purpose of this wedding!" Agatha argued but Sera wasn't listening.

"Two weddings are better anyway—just ask your sisters. Now I only had one, and I think I would have liked two," Sera replied as she walked back into the living room, announcing that the other wedding was still on.

"What just happened?" Chris asked her as she shook her head against his chest.

"I got outsmarted. I worked so hard on this. I even wore my good shirt." She pointed at it but didn't pull away from him.

"Is it so bad to marry me twice?" He wanted to laugh at her but managed to control it, just barely.

"Doves, Chris," she stated, her grip on him not loosening.

Pulling her free of him, he set her back on the counter. After kissing her nose, he asked, "Are you ready to start our two-day wedding celebration?"

"This is not happening to me," Agatha grumbled.

"This could only happen to you. To us. We wasted most of our lives to get to this day, so let's make it an event. Bring on the top hats and the doves and whatever your mom throws at us. It's nothing compared to what we've gone through to get here." He stepped away and lifted her off the counter.

Agatha took a deep breath once she was on her feet. "Can I just have a second to get emotionally ready for this?"

"Of course, Agatha Christie Lovely. But you know the moment you walk back out there, we get to get married. For the first time," he said, because he was ready to start this life with her. No matter what life brought their way, they were in it together.

"Okay, I know," she said and took another breath. He knew this was out of her comfort zone. All of it. But he also knew she was ready. Their days of sabotaging themselves were over. They were destined to find each other again and again until they got it right.

Walking out of the kitchen, he stopped at the door and looked back at her. He loved looking at her and knowing she was his. She must have sensed it because she turned to him and smiled.

Turning around, he walked back and tucked her hair behind her ears and whispered the first thing that came to his mind. "Hey, Chris."

Smiling at him, she replied, "Hey, Chris."

Kissing her forehead, he added, "I love you."

This was his past, present, and future all rolled up in one package. In a few minutes, she would be his wife. Then again tomorrow, she would be his wife again. And who knew what the day after would bring. Nothing but surprises and happiness lay ahead of them. Forever.

EPILOGUE

"I CANNOT BELIEVE that you forgot diapers, again," Agatha hissed at Chris as she adjusted Christie on her lap. At three months, the baby was the spitting image of her sister but had a rather Agatha-like personality.

"I cannot believe you're blaming this on me! I am not in charge of diaper bags." He was trying to get Poppy to stop running away from him. At three, she was a terror and hated being confined.

"Because you don't ever look at it until we're away from the house. That means I have to do everything," she argued, even if she couldn't really be mad at him when he was wearing a T-shirt that had her little sister's name on it. The shirt was maybe a bit too small, but she enjoyed the way his biceps stretched the sleeves so deliciously. He didn't even argue when she gave it to him to wear that morning, probably because everyone else in the family had one. How else could they embarrass Emma at her graduation without saying a word?

"Stop fighting, you two. Because if your only issue is not enough diapers, I can assure you there's a Lovely baby in every damn size around here." Harper slapped them both on the back of the head from behind.

Agatha had no way of arguing back; it was true. From Poppy down to Buzz's newborn, Lark, they had the spectrum of baby butts covered. The Lovelys had enjoyed a baby boom. It seemed once everyone had married, they started to have kids. Even Cliff and Dr. Maby had a baby not long before Christie had been born. The only holdout was Harper, who was steadfast in her refusal to even talk about having one of her own. Agatha knew it was more her lack of success in getting pregnant that she was unwilling to talk about, and since her catering business was booming, Harper was focusing on that.

"Shut up, Harper. That isn't the point here," Agatha said to her sister.

"Emma is graduating, you turds. Pay attention." Harper stood up and took Poppy from Chris's lap. Her goal now was being the best aunt, and she was more than happy to hold any baby she could for as long as they let her. That and spoiling them all rotten and telling the kids that their parents don't love them like she did.

Chris turned and waved at their daughter, but Agatha knew the kid wasn't paying attention anymore. With a grunt, he rested his arm on the back of her chair, making small circles on her bare shoulder.

"This is our first graduation together," he whispered in her ear.

"You're right. You have never taken me to one of these before. I should be upset," she teased him, still loving their closeness after eighteen months together. Agatha knew she would never tire of being the center of his attention.

"You missed out on ours, Ag, the one where we could have sat together and made out," he said with a smirk.

Agatha nudged him in the side with her elbow. "I think that would have gotten us kicked out of graduation, and therefore, making being here for Emma's impossible." Her eyes went to the graduates and found Emma's head in the crowd. Her little sister was the first Lovely since Mabel to graduate with honors. Though she would never admit to liking school, she had flourished there. Very un-Lovely of her.

"Worth it, but you're right as usual. I would have just held your hand and stared at you with dreamy eyes." He took it and held it, even if she couldn't hold his back because of baby Christie in her arms.

She leaned into him and whispered, "I do believe you were drunk that day, so I wouldn't have held your hand, and your eyes would have been glassy."

"How do you know that?" He sat up straight and looked at her.

"I might have attended, just not walked. Couldn't miss Christopher Lowell getting his diploma, could I? Not after all the years I knew you." She leaned her head onto his shoulder and kissed his chin.

The feeling that this was the man she would spend the rest of her life with hadn't dissipated yet. In fact, it had grown every day since she had fallen for him. It wasn't even the big moments that brought her the most joy; it was the little ones. Getting up in the night together with Christie, watching cartoons over and over on the couch with Poppy, rushing to the door when he came home from work, falling into bed exhausted at the end of the day, together.

That was all she had ever wanted in life: the little things. And to do them all with the man she loved by her side, knowing that he loved her as much as she loved him. Happy in their simple life together.

THE WIND PUSHED a lock of black hair across her face, and he instantly put it behind her ear, still loving to touch her after eighteen months and two kids. It still bothered him that he had missed so many years with her, though his life would have been much different if they had actually gotten together after the party. He knew he wouldn't have led the same crazy life. She was his ground, as he was hers.

When Christie had been born, they had oddly agreed to name her after her mom, or as Agatha said, after him. Agreeing to disagree, they had just told anyone who asked it was a family name. The only one who had not liked the name had been Violet, who called her Plum because it was a color.

With Christie, he had finally gotten to nurture his child and watch her grow. Every day of it had been amazing for him to witness. Agatha's second pregnancy had been just as good as the first. She had wanted to keep it from her family until she was well past the point she had miscarried years before but had slipped up. Or she had told Poppy, who was more than willing to tell everyone else.

Now with two girls, he was on his way to a full house of women, which Agatha was more than on board with. He knew she still missed her sisters living in the house, though she was happy that each had found love. She was happier now that she had as well.

Saturday morning was still breakfast with the girls, though men were now invited if they wanted to attend, and children were always welcome. As far as Chris knew, there hadn't been a black eye in almost a year, though bruises were still common occurrences.

He kissed her temple. "I found your diploma and framed it for your office."

"Why?" She turned to him in confusion.

"Because my wife needed something for her office walls." Taking the baby from her arms, he settled her into his lap. She was sound asleep with her thumb in her mouth, her dark hair was, as usual, sticking straight into the air around her head. At three months old, he was sure she wasn't going to have the curls of her sister, but she still reminded him adorably of Agatha.

Straightening the blanket around Christie, Agatha whispered, "I don't need the office, Chris. I do my bills at the table like humans, and the rest takes care of itself."

Chuckling at her answer, he said, "The rest is a company. You're not just an artist anymore; you're a company. The president needs an office."

He wasn't going to mention that "the rest" as she called it usually sat on the kitchen table, ignored, until she absolutely had to do it. Then she looked at the paperwork and complained. Luckily, they still had enough extra bedrooms that she could use one as an office.

The last time he had brought the idea up, she had said she needed them as bedrooms for her sisters. No one had slept over for over a year, but that night, all of Agatha's sisters had stayed the night. Not that it had proved her point; it just proved how stubborn his wife was and to what lengths her sisters would go for her.

But an office was needed. Since getting married, she had released five more books in her little series, and they had been instant hits. A few times she had even gone on book signing tours. She grumbled about it but secretly loved that people liked her books as much as she did.

"I just like to draw, Chris. Not the rest. I am not a president. I think I'm going to hire Buzz to be president." She glanced at her sister, who was once again pregnant and miserable. Even Jonas had to admit his wife complained a bit too much during pregnancy, though Chris was sure that had gotten back to Buzz based on how attentive Jonas had been lately.

Reaching up, he touched his wife's cheek. "Except you've been working that end since you started, and you've been doing great at it. More than great. You don't need Buzz. Quit hiding behind a sour attitude, Ag. It doesn't work with me."

"It should." She huffed and crossed her arms, turning back to the valedictorian speaking on the stage.

"It never will again; I'm on to you. Poppy gets her personality right from you." He kissed her cheek, which caused to smile, but she didn't turn to him.

"Not a chance. That is all her grandma," she argued as if he hadn't lived with her long enough to know her inside and out.

He kissed her again. "It comes from you, and I love that you're still hiding it from your entire family. Though they have been catching on."

"I don't think so. I'm pretty good at telling them what I want them to know," Agatha stated, and Chris knew that at least half of her sisters had heard what she said.

"Stop fighting. Can't you just enjoy Emma's day?" Sera turned from the row in front of them and gave them a death glare, one that instantly melted before she reached back and took the baby out of Chris's arms, which was perfectly fine with him. Then he had two hands to touch his wife. He slipped one over the back of her chair, and with the other, he took her hand and pulled her close. She settled into him and sighed.

While making lazy circles on her bare arm, he toyed with the wedding ring and promise ring she wore every day. They sparkled in the sunshine as he counted the red stones on the ring, one for each year wasted as they grew up together but apart.

Pulling her close, he kissed her forehead and whispered, "Hey, Chris."

"Hey, Chris." She covered his hand with hers and squeezed.

"Happy Graduation, Agatha Christie." And he smiled when she wrinkled her nose at her name, then turned her attention to the stage as Emma's name was called.

As one, the entire family jumped to their feet and cheered. Chris took the moment of confusion to kiss his wife and make out at a graduation. He was never going to regret not doing something again when it involved Agatha, or Chris, or Christie, or whoever she wanted to be. Not ever again.

BONUS EPILOGUE

A Cher song started playing slightly louder than Agatha liked, but she instantly stopped working and set the black pencil down. She was still slightly disappointed it was just black and not charcoal or some cooler name. But the bear had to be black, so black he was.

Agatha hummed along to the music as she straightened her easel for the evening. She wouldn't get back up to her studio that day, nor would she until her alarm went off at four in the morning since her best working time was still when everyone slept.

Heading down the stairs, she stopped on the second floor and went into her room. After years of marriage, it reflected Chris's tastes more than hers. It seemed his tastes ran heavily toward throw pillows. He bought them every chance he got. But then again, they didn't last long on their bed.

Grabbing the card off the dresser, she headed down the last flight of stairs to see Chris sitting in the nearly dark living room, the only light was the flickering of a football game on the TV. Agatha only glanced at it on her way past. Football still wasn't an interest of hers, and after all these years, she knew it never would be.

Kissing his head, she looked at the sleeping baby in his arms, another girl. Chris's wish to have a house full of girls was happening.

Penn made number four, and even if she was still less then a year old, he was already hinting at another.

"Are you heading out?" he whispered, not wanting to wake Penn from her sleep. Of all their babies, she was the most difficult. Agatha blamed it on the blonde curls on her head. After all, like daddy, like daughter.

"Yes, Mom said ten. I really have no idea why these things have to happen so late at night," she grumbled, knowing that if they met up any sooner in the evening, someone was bound to bring a child. Sometimes the sisters liked to get together without their children.

"What happened to the woman I met who went to bed at dawn? Where did she go?" Chris looked around the room with a grin.

"Shut up. That was before these kids started waking me up at dawn," she complained. Not that she would trade being a mom for any amount of money or sleep, but she missed sleeping in. She really missed sleeping in with her husband, or not sleeping. She missed not sleeping with her husband.

"Let me lay her down before you leave." Chris shimmied off the couch and rushed up the stairs.

Agatha slowly slipped on her tennis shoes and her jacket. It was only a short walk to her mom's, but the evening was chilly. Or it had been a few hours before.

She heard him come down the stairs again as she was zipping up her coat in near darkness. She wasn't ready when he pinned her to the wall and started kissing her neck.

"Don't go. They're all asleep," he growled as his hand slipped under her coat and shirt, cupping her breasts.

"Chris." She tried not to moan but failed.

He bit her collarbone lightly. "Stay."

"I have to go, I missed last week's," she argued weakly. This was why she had missed last week. The sex against that very wall had been worth it.

"Miss it again. I need to taste you," he said hoarsely into her neck as his hands did things to her breast that she would never tire of.

"We've been married for years; I taste the same." She half-heart-edly tried to push him away and failed.

"You're my drug, woman." He ran his tongue over the sensitive spot on her neck.

"I have to go, but I'll come home in like an hour. Stay awake." She moaned but tried to keep her resolve strong.

He pushed her shirt up as he sank to his knees. "I can't let you go."

"An hour, and I'll do that thing you like." She ran her fingers through his hair, still curly and still perfectly soft in her hands.

He stopped and looked up at her. "Which one?"

She ran a finger over his lips. Knowing she would do anything he asked, even if he asked her to do it right now. After all, she saw her sisters all the time. "Whichever one you ask for."

"Go, but hurry home, and I'll do that thing *you* like." He stood up and zipped her jacket himself.

"Which one?" She raised in eyebrow in question.

"Every. Single. One. Of. Them." He kissed her between each word then with a groan he let her go.

She headed out the door and down the street in the chilly night. The snow was finally gone, but the chill was still there. She was surprised how quiet the street was. None of her sisters were waiting for her at Sera's house. Both Sera and Mabel still lived on their street; which meant that her other sisters usually parked by Sera's house and walked since it was closer to the bar.

Pushing her way into the door of The Grog, Agatha decided that she loved that it looked the exact same it had the first time she had walked in as a teenager. The tables and booths were all in the same location, and the bar was still stocked with the same alcohol she used to serve. Every time she walked in, she was happy she wasn't going into work there anymore. Thanks to the success of her books, she never would again.

Going first to the bar, she ordered her usual from Emma, who was bartending that night. She was still in college working toward her law degree, much to her mother's delight. Not that Sera would say anything to her older kids about it. She was simply happy her oldest was set on a more traditional track than the others. Violet, at fifteen, was a completely different; more Lovely than the rest of them put together.

Sliding the birthday card over to her sister, she knew they would have a party soon to celebrate. After all, she was Sera's daughter, no matter how old she got. But sometimes she liked to have a moment between just the two of them to remember the connection they had enjoyed when Agatha had been her second mom. Since they had moved out, they were not as close as they had once been, but no matter how old Emma and Violet got, they were still her little sisters.

Emma thanked her with a huge hug; she was Sera's, after all. Then they chatted about this and that, and Agatha's eyes went to the corner, their usual spot. Everyone was already there.

Maby and Lucy were sitting side by side, practically touching. The twin connection never wore off, it seemed. Lucy had been thinking about going back to work when the twins went to school. Her older girls were either out of the house or old enough to not need her. That was, until when the twins had turned four, and she accidentally got pregnant again. Little Juliet was now two, and Lucy hadn't mentioned working again.

With only two kids, Maby and Cliff were not nearly as busy as the Montgomery's. CJ was six and so much like his dad, it was scary. At two years old, Mabel Lucie Lovely Montgomery reminded Agatha so much of her dad, and Lovy was always the center of attention wherever she went. Neither of them started reading early, much to Maby's annoyance.

Across from them, Harper threw a handful of popcorn at Agatha and Emma. She and Kaine were not having kids, and she was more than willing to tell anyone who asked. Their argument was that they had more than enough nieces and nephews, so adding more kids would be too much. It was probably the truth since Kaine's sister Arabella had just had their sixth, even after her wife had said there would be a hard stop at three, then four, then five. Agatha was excited to see how far Arabella could push the other woman. Probably to ten, easily.

But Agatha knew that Harper had fertility issues that the couple hadn't been able to resolve. It wasn't something that she willingly talked about with everyone, but Agatha hoped they would look into other avenues to have children. Harper would be an amazing mother.

Sera yelled something at Harper, probably telling her to leave her sisters alone, like always. Since everyone had gotten married, she had stopped acting like their mom all the time, only when it was needed. After Benji was born, she and Harrison had either decided not to have another one, or it just worked out that way. So Benji had been completely spoiled by everyone in the house.

Buzz and Jonas ended up with three little rugrats, and Buzz was hinting at another, but Jonas was saying no. But that was probably because she usually spent months complaining while pregnant that her pregnancies always seemed to last years. Where Buzz had always floundered at keeping a job, she was an amazing mom, involved and dedicated to her kids and their activities. Sometimes, Agatha had to admit it was what she was destined to become as well. She had even taken in Louisa and Frankie when they needed a place or just a family.

No one had seen their mother since she and George had moved to Belize. They hadn't been back, and not one of their children had been down to see them. Not that anyone cared. Maybe her two younger daughters did, but neither Frankie or Louisa ever said anything about it.

When Emma had started college, she had insisted she would not live at home, even if she was going to the college Maby taught at. So, in true Sera style, she had Harrison buy a house for their daughter. Not just any house; it was directly across the street from her parents. It wasn't the independence Emma had wanted, but it was her own house.

Within months, she had rented the additional four bedrooms to her friends. When that failed, Louisa and Frankie had moved in with her. Then Alexis and Aubrey had also moved in, which meant there were quite a few Lovelys still on their street. Sometimes it was too many, and sometimes it wasn't enough, but no matter the number, Agatha was happy to have her family close by.

Heading over to the table, Agatha was greeted her sisters' teasing with happiness. Some things never changed, even when they hadn't lived together in years.

"Where did you find that shirt?" Harper stood up and demanded as Agatha got to the table.

Agatha looked down. The shirt was deep purple with neon green writing that said, "Taxass." Five years before, the shirt supply sort of dwindled down to just the "Grand Cannon" shirts in odd sizes, so Agatha started to make new ones. Either nobody had noticed or cared, but they still loved the shirts and always wore them. Even Lucy, who was probably the only one who knew they were not hers.

"Bottom of a box in the basement," she lied as she sat down, slipping her jacket off completely.

"I want it." Harper could barely get the words out before Maby tried to claim it. "Not a chance, Mabs, mine."

"I want yours then," Sera stated. Harper was wearing her favorite yellow "Yellin Stan" shirt, a shirt that still made the rounds even if they didn't live together anymore.

"No, I want both." Harper hugged herself, or maybe the shirt.

"That's not how it works. I need a shirt!" Agatha argued.

"Choose, Harper! I get the other." Buzz started pulling off her shirt as she said it.

"Fudge! That one!" Harper panicked and picked Agatha's shirt.

"I want Buzz's," Maby stated, pointing at Buzz's blue "Kantaky" shirt. Another classic.

"Then I get Lucy's. It's been a while since I went "Grand Cannon." Harrison's going to just laugh," Sera said, already pulling off her shirt.

"I should have done laundry today, but I was so busy. This was the last clean shirt I had," Lucy explained, but happily removed the shirt and tossed it at Sera.

"You should hire out the laundry." Buzz held out her shirt as she took Harper's yellow one, always willing to spend her husband's money to make her life better. Though it had taken years for her to start.

"I'm a stay-at-home mom. That's my job." Lucy took Sera's shirt and pulled it on.

"You have the money, Luce. Then you would have clothes also."

Agatha pulled off her shirt and tossed it at Harper, who slid it on, ran her hand over it and grinned. Agatha grabbed Maby's red "Witchit-tahhh" shirt, one she had made a year before and still really liked. It was not a very Lucy-like mistake, but it was funny since the tahhh was on the second line of the shirt.

"Everyone dressed?" Emma asked, bringing over a tray of drinks.

"That did not happen, Emmaline." Sera blushed, as if their swapping didn't actually happen every week, and her daughter was there to witness it most the time.

"Okay, Sera. It's never happened before." Emma handed out the drinks as she grinned at her mom. Sera might get some of her kids to believe she wasn't just as wild as everyone else, but Emma knew too much.

"And it will never happen again." The sisters laughed. They all knew their swapping would continue happening forever.

All the sisters were happy and settled, had been for so long it was sometimes hard to remember how wild they had been once upon a time. Agatha leaned back and had to admit that no matter what she had thought at the time, she was happy to have been a part of it.

The End

Thank you so much for reading Falling into a Second Chance.

ABOUT ALIE GARNETT

I love to read and prefer a little spice in those books. I am lucky enough to live on a small hobby farm in northern Minnesota with her husband and two kids. I enjoy spending time in the pasture with my two mini horses and one fainting goat (who doesn't actually faint). When I'm not writing, I'm busy trying to do all the things I didn't get to while writing. Or maybe I wouldn't have gotten to them anyway, because its laundry, dishes and fun things like that.

ALSO BY ALIE GARNETT

<u>Indulge</u>

Craving Winter

Enticing Aurora

<u>Landstad, ND</u>

Invisible

Irresistible

Impulsive

Insuppressible

Intriguing

Imperfect

Irreplaceable

<u>The Great Lovely Falls</u>

Falling for the Single Mom

Falling for his Best Friends Sister

Falling for the Boss

Falling for his Step-Sister

Falling for his Fake Wife

Falling into a Second Chance

<u>Hart Series</u>

Seeing her Pain

Her Favor

Max Valentine is Looking at Me!

Keeping her Safe

<u>Stand Alone</u>

Romancing the Doctor